VIIVI LUIK (b. 1946) is one of the most highly-acclaimed and well-known writers in Estonia today. She has been a freelance writer since 1968, and has published eleven collections of poetry, several children's books, and three novels. *Seitsmes rahukevad* (The Seventh Spring of Peace) was published in 1985, and depicts rural life in 1950s Estonia through the eyes of a child. *Ajaloo ilu – The Beauty of History* – was first published in 1991. Her books have been translated into a dozen languages: this is the first time her work has been published in English. (See www.viiviluik. ee)

HILDI HAWKINS is a translator and editor based in London. She was for many years the London editor of *Books from Finland* and has co-edited or co-written a wide variety of books. She is also an editor of the journal *things* (www. thingsmagazine.net). In 2006 she was awarded the Finnish Government's Prize for Literary Translation.

RICHARD C. M. MOLE is a senior lecturer in the politics of Central Europe at the UCL School of Slavonic and Eastern European Studies (SSEES) in London. He is the author of *The Baltic States. From the Soviet Union to the European Union* (Routledge, 2012).

Some other books from Norvik Press

Juhani Aho: *The Railroad* (translated by Owen Witesman)

Jens Bjørneboe: *Moment of Freedom* (translated by Esther Greenleaf Mürer)

Jens Bjørneboe: *Powderhouse* (translated by Esther Greenleaf Mürer)

Jens Bjørneboe: *The Silence* (translated by Esther Greenleaf Mürer)

Jógvan Isaksen: *Walpurgis Tide* (translated by John Keithsson)

Svava Jakobsdóttir: *Gunnlöth's Tale* (translated by Oliver Watts)

Christopher Moseley (ed.): *From Baltic Shores*

Henry Parland: *To Pieces* (translated by Dinah Cannell)

Hanne Marie Svendsen: *Under the Sun* (translated by Marina Allemano)

Edith Södergran: *The Poet Who Created Herself: Selected Letters of Edith Södergran* (translated by Silvester Mazzarella)

Anton Tammsaare: *The Misadventures of the New Satan* (translated by Olga Shartze and Christopher Moseley)

Marie Wells (ed.): *The Discovery of Nineteenth-Century Scandinavia*

THE BEAUTY OF HISTORY

A Novel

by

Viivi Luik

Translated from the Estonian by
Hildi Hawkins

with an Afterword by
Richard C. M. Mole

Norvik Press
2016

Originally published in Estonian by Eesti Raamat under the title of *Ajaloo ilu* (1991)
© Viivi Luik

This translation © Hildi Hawkins 2007

The translator's moral right to be identified as the translator of the work has been asserted.

Afterword © Richard C. M. Mole 2007

A catalogue record for this book is available from the British Library.
ISBN: 978-1-909408-27-2

First published in 2007 by Norvik Press, University of East Anglia, Norwich NR4 7TJ. This edition first published in 2016.

Norvik Press gratefully acknowledges the generous support of the Estonian Cultural Endowment and the Stephen Spender Memorial Trust towards the publication of this translation.

Norvik Press
Department of Scandinavian Studies
University College London
Gower Street
London WC1E 6BT
United Kingdom

Website: www.norvikpress.com
E-mail address: norvik.press@ucl.ac.uk

Managing editors: Elettra Carbone, Sarah Death, Janet Garton, C. Claire Thomson.

Cover illustration: *Black Pearl and Its Shell*. Photographer: TheBrockenInaGlory.

Cover design: Elettra Carbone

Printed in the UK by Lightning Source UK Ltd.

Contents

The Beauty of History

* * *

* * *

1

Toward evening, the sky rises higher and takes on its true form. It becomes a dome and a vault. With strange and threatening self-evidence it encompasses military district headquarters, militia stations and passport offices. Those who are trapped beneath this vault cannot escape.

The same vault encompasses the Rusalka statue in Tallinn, and the platforms and railway bridges of Riga. With equal indifference it encompasses potato fields and apple orchards, frontier posts and barracks. Down in the south, spruce forests slowly give way to beech. Up in the north are the Arctic Sea and the White Sea Canal, whose building demanded more *human sacrifices* than we can imagine. Up there, too, is the Karelian isthmus, where the bones of the Winter War dead still lie. Down in the mountains are Dracula's castle and Ceausescu's kingdom. Among the black beech-trunks on the mountainsides weave great clouds of fog, like sleep and smoke.

Something is happening. Secret commands pass along cables, through air, water and earth. Paper fears the light. Among spruce and beech forests, wheatfields and graves, old steppes, wind and approaching darkness, stand human dwellings. Pale apples glow in the trees, their seeds already brown. Grain ripens.

What is going on in the wide world? What is Brezhnev doing? Does he feast on butter and honey, and at night does he sleep between furs? And does he work, and does he play? What is happening really? And where?

No one utters a sound. Silence stretches from the coast of the Arctic Sea right down to the river Danube. Only newspapers rustle. The gloomy lustre of evening still flows over lost kingdoms in which, even now, people live, although walls have ears. Aunt Olga saw the great famine with her own eyes. It is not true that farmhouses were filled with corpses and set alight, as some people say. At first people still crawled, then each died where he was. On that very spot. Before they died, they howled. The official name of this great famine was an *emergency*. The *emergency* zone was sealed off. It was kept secret. Who brought Aunt Olga out is not known. Olga was given a dead person's sugar to lick, but why the dead person had sugar, or why he did not lick it himself while he was alive, or who the dead person really was, that, too, is unknown.

Now there is no hunger! Now any kitchen maid can lead the state! The main thing is that there should be no war!*

Sem was able to leave, but Anna had to teach the murderer to read. Grandfather's grave is in New York. In some places there are still graves. In the drawers are black envelopes containing photographs and even letters.

The curtain stirs. The dark allure of evening is born of foreign languages. The telephone sputters and growls by itself. A thick green sofa cushion has been thrown on top of it. No point in asking why. It will become clear. The leaves of the trees, on the other side of the window, look black, as if they were made of iron. The air is full of the smoke and fire of summer. It feels as though the leaves do not rustle, but rumble. Their rumbling fills the whole city. It forces its way in through the window and stifles all the words that are spoken tonight. You can try to remember them as much as you like, but they remain hidden forever beneath a dark, iron rumbling. They are not Estonian words. Or, more precisely – they are not words of your mother tongue.

She sits in the middle of the high evening room and allows the hand of another, the hand of a man, to feel her chin, her skull. The hand is young but experienced. Familiar with bones, like that of a surgeon, or of the angel of the day of judgement, who raises the dead. She gazes with concealed interest at the undefined clay

---

* Refers to note on page 141.

8

creature tended by the man's skilful hands, as it gradually begins to come to life. With a sense of strangeness, she watches the spirit enter it. The eyes have been remodelled many times, and the tip of the nose. The ears, too, have been remade. *Her* eyelids, *her* nose, *her* ears. She is surprised that he can make *her* out of clay. She looks on, swinging her legs. Only at midday she had been sceptical, sure in herself that it was not possible to copy *her*, that the spirit could not enter her image. Her arrogance doubtless stems from the fact that the Lord has not yet instructed his angel to soak whips in brine for her. The Lord is still waiting and watching.

But at the same time she follows the movements of the other, accompanying them with her eyes, gazes intently, scrutinises them, as boldly and minutely as a child observes a visitor. All day she has watched him make the clay figure, but realises only now that he really exists.

Looking into his eyes, she sees in them only now something that surprises and enchants her. She sees there her own image, and only that. Not clay, but flesh. She sees the forty-eight kilos of flesh and bone within which existence demands more courage and fortitude than one could imagine. One must have spirit; or, at least, a machine. More likely a machine, for machines become more and more precious and they must be looked after more and more tenderly. Machines may be, even should be, loved!

Nevertheless, she has already finished writing two books, and suspects dimly that words must be soaked in blood in order to be effective; but this must be done in such high secrecy that no one for God's sake should understand what exactly has happened to them. She has sold words, and thrown them away; she bears the same name as later, but now it sounds different. It is a twenty-one-year-old's name. People taste it, smack their lips, and wait to hear what others say. Such games pass her by; she does not even notice them. She comes through them untouched.

She wants to stand in the light, but wants also to see what is in the dark corners. Red stars and swastikas attract her like people's eyes and what can be seen in them. When she sees a rose, she

9

desires to eat it. She has eaten many roses. She knows exactly what a dandelion tastes like, and apple blossom. That the taste of lilac is bitter is also known by the entire people of Estonia. Every year, as lilacs flower beside sheds and potato stores like emissaries from strange worlds, it feels as if a deathly silence, the silence described by survivors in their memoirs, is descending over Tallinn and Tartu. The sweeter the smell of the lilac and the bluer the glimmer of the sky, the more perilous it feels to remain in the Baltic republics. No one knows, of these republics, whether they really exist. Life in them is incomprehensible and mysterious. Here, fifty years are the mere twinkling of an eye; they are a dream, a mist, which hides ruins and empty foundations. A sparkling spring breeze, here, can blow life into the bones of the dead and lift them up from the depths of the grave. The evil one has been heard here in broad daylight giving a radio talk. Seeing lilacs, here, one never knows whether they are flowering now, or years ago, or whether they are only the image of longing, which can be seen even on the other side of the border.

At night, here, people lie awake. Ears are pricked, listening in case the evil one comes.

The lilac flowers in its usual way; in place of the old, liquidated government a new one appears, and holds its sessions once more.

She has played unconcernedly all her life, with images and words, against the background of the history of the Baltic countries. She treats the myths of Greece and Rome like a sales catalogue from which to select gods. No god pleases her enough to satisfy her completely. Always she has flicked through the book, from one end to the other and back again, studying all the pictures, ready to take something from each god. A crafty smile from one, winged feet from another. She studies the gods' knees and mouths like parts of a bicycle that she is unable to assemble into a new and better bike.

As already mentioned, the Angel of the Lord has not yet soaked whips in brine for her.

Now, however, it is only August 1968. The parquet clicks, a

floor-draught drives dust from under the bookshelves and redwood chairs. It whirls in the centre of the floor like a grey wisp. In two hours' time she ought to catch the train, and the train, with dramatic howls and dull shudders, will take her through Valmiera and Cesis and Sigulda and Valga and Tartu and back to Tallinn.

The more thoroughly he takes the measure of her bones, the more it interests her, for no one has looked at her bones with such greed and self-absorption. No one has yet wanted to use her bones to solve the riddle of his own life, or tried to reproduce them, like the bones of a god, in clay, wood or stone.

Her head is tilted like a dog's, she tries to make out the other's words and conceal the fact that she understands nothing. The expression 'delo v tom'* causes her particular confusion. She has heard it many times, and even read it, but nevertheless she cannot say what it means. There are many other mysterious words. She is certain that she knows the world of words through and through, down to its sombre depths, but it turns out that one only has to make a train journey of a couple of hundred kilometres and that world disappears like blue smoke. A train journey of a couple of hundred kilometres can make a person as dumb as an animal.

'Why don't we speak German?' he asks impatiently, but the German language is hidden in the darkness of her skull, and will not come out on command. She has never yet had to *speak* German. She has done written exercises. She can write, without error, 'Der grosse, bunte, fettige Hahn sieht nach links und nach rechts und kräht lauter', and 'Wenn der Morgen schön ist, geht der Onkel zur Arbeit zu Fuss'.

So talking does not come to much at first, and they must get used to this. They must learn to say much in few words. It looks as if life has made a poignant demand of them, but luckily they do not themselves understand it. The colour of the trees' leaves turns completely black, the great city holds its breath, it is time for the radio news; evening is really here.

It does not concern her. To her, his name does not seem in the

11

least literary or hackneyed, only very strange. Lion. On the telephone, Lev. Why, has not been discussed. Until now, she has not known a single Jew, apart from an immigrant teacher whose son was a book-keeper at the sawmill. As a child she observed both the teacher and the sawmill book-keeper, but did not see anything that might hint at an unusual connection with Jesus, who was betrayed, and Judas, who received thirty pieces of silver for the betrayal. The book-keeper had a picture of Stalin on his cigarette case, and it was said that it was this that protected him from persecution. The teacher, his mother, had an old, yellow poodle and could have knitted a pullover from its hair for anyone who did not mind the smell of dogs. She also sold goat's milk, which no one bought. Could she be connected with Jehovah, who is thy god? Or Jesus, who was dead, buried and rose again on the third day from the dead and ascended to heaven, where he sits on the right hand of God, his father, and shall come again just when he is no longer expected?

What connection could Lion have with those people, and what is there about him that is strange or special? One thing is certain – he should drop his eyes if he does not want them to betray him, particularly in a country in which his name is Lev! So, first, his eyes. Then, his skin. Even the maiden of olden times who bathed by moonlight would have been proud of such skin. His blood shines through it like embers. It is quite possible that the smell of blood, too, permeates the skin, and wafts through this room like an invisible red curtain. If there was a cat here, it would detect the pulsating vein in the bare neck at once and begin to stalk it. But what about her, what is she doing?

Studying the other's eyes and skin, she sneezes, for the room is full of dust and the smell of damp clay. She has looked at all there is to look at in the other's face, and now it does not interest her any longer, for at this moment she would like to be back in Tallinn, recounting what it was like in Riga. She wants to be, once again, the master of words, not their servant. For that, she need only travel three hundred kilometres up toward the north. There she would make of today a myth. This day would then be under control. With the help of words, she would make its every aspect visible and harmless.

She imagines regions and places where she could be now, but is not. She sees herself telling the *longhairs* a new myth about her own clay image. Perhaps she will add, flattered, flattered in spite of herself, that the sculpture will be in an exhibition. But perhaps she will keep it to herself. Her imagination is very vivid – she does not forget to paint in the background, peopling it with the café's regular customers, the old ladies at the corner tables, irritably munching cakes. She has the waitresses bustling and the light streaming through the big window as waitresses are in the habit of bustling and light of streaming. She intends to steal from the Latvian writer Skalbe a sentence about the river Daugava. The sentence runs: 'In the Daugava swam a great fish.' She would have nothing to say in Tallinn about the trees' ominous rumbling, for she has not yet really noticed it, although it is true that from time to time she listens for something.

Her gaze is like still water. But she changes her expressions so thoroughly that it is as if at the same time she changed the colour of her eyes and her line of destiny. Looking at her more closely, willow-whistles, bare feet, flax and rye might come to mind; or, equally, innocent babies and complete charlatans, whose broad smiles are like the wings of birds – unexpectedly spreading open, then folding shut in full flight.

This gives a suspicious impression of her, and compels one to give her a sharp second glance. She has cut her hair herself above her eyebrows, and her khaki epauletted shirt is rather threadbare. Its back has faded and is far lighter than the front. She even has a wide leather belt, as do the *others*, as do all who are drinking in the air of this year and changing the street scenes of the capitals. Her belt she has wheedled out of a Tartu boy called Genoveva.

Under the chair lie her sandals, whose straps cut her bare toes like a knife. (But only when she has walked two kilometres. She has measured this accurately.) Little by little, her blood has stiffened the straps. She should soak them in spirits and soften them with the back of an axe!

13

She reads the news in other people's clothes as in the newspapers, knows the meaning of tennis shoes daubed with felt pen or a simple flower drawn on the back of a shirt. Anyone with short hair, to her, is empty space. Lion *does* have short hair. You can even see his ear-lobes. It is also true that, this morning, Lion sized up her sandals and epauletted shirt with a certain and completely understandable mistrust; but equally, she herself deeply despised Lion's soft woollen jumper with its label, 'Pure Wool Reine Wolle'. To her, such garments are for *old men.* Nevertheless, it caught her eye, and she would like very much to sell it in a *komission.** Secretly, she wonders why he has not done so already, and used the money to buy halva or jam turnovers. She has no idea of his uncle in New York, his grandfather's grave, or even what the word OVIR* means; and he has no real conception of cheap jam turnovers, or even of what *a lot of money* is. A hundred roubles is a lot of money.

He cannot even guess that less than three hundred kilometres away are villages and old provincial towns, fields and meadows above which, even on the most dazzling summer's day, black whirls from the wing of the Angel of Death. That through bogs and swamps, cow pastures and overgrown horse-pens, wind narrow, white roads.

That suddenly a sharp church-tower pierces the sky and you are in Estonia, in the village of Kolga-Jaan, where, one hundred years ago, in a lost grave, old Ell of Long-Michael was buried, who collected urine and dog-fat and stinging-nettles, caught an incubus in the act, shouted 'Hands up!', and scourged its plump white housewifely bottom with a holy rowan whip until the blood flowed.

Quite close to Kolga-Jaan, in 1923, a living pike was found in a cradle in place of a child, its jaws wide open and eyes in its head like a baron's. With her own ears the old woman of the house heard a murmuring from under the saucepan: 'Splash blood in the porridge! Splash blood in the porridge!' In front of the old fire-station, Einar and Oskar can still be seen. But Einar has been pinned to the threshing floor of the drying barn with a bayonet through the neck. All that remained of Oskar on the battlefield was a charred finger-joint and his sooty Song Notebook. Written sprawlingly with a blunt pencil were the words:

> Return for us now there is not
> Ahead certain only the fall;
> Small price for Estonia's freedom
> The death that awaits us all.

> Chorus:
> The fire may temper our weapons
> But the evil one laughs from the flames
> Ha-ha hah-hah-hah ha...*

But that cannot hold back the coming of the future. In the future, in the village of Kolga-Jaan, too, people will have to crowd into the shop to buy pigs' ears and moth-eaten flour, *because what can you do, you have to buy, otherwise you can just get up on the table yourself when the children come home from school whining for food.*

In the future people's faces, in Kolga-Jaan, too, will be mistrustful and submissive, long accustomed to intimidation. In the future, Estonians' milk-pails and teapots will begin to be decorated with the incomprehensible and mysterious threat, 'Nu pogodi',* written in Cyrillic characters.

Nevertheless, the old, stubborn violet and wood anemone, globeflower and primrose, bent grass and camomile still appear always anew, as if the bulldozer had not buried them forever under clay and earth. Huge reflections of the sky gleam in the black water of the river's deeps, and in their light even the expensive new pig-farm, with all its dung and urine, is as nothing.

The potato is sown in May, and harvested in September. In July it flowers. Its purple and white flowers decorate the field's furrows as if they were grave-mounds under which are buried history and a great forgetting. Yellowed notebooks and diaries

15

found in bunkers and trenches express no more than the melancholy of the twilight above the black spruces.

The yellow butterflies of April flutter once a year above the burnt-out clearings and collapsed bunkers like the verses of a folk-song. It is not known whence they come, or where the wind will take them.

Concerning how, in Prague tonight, shadows move on ceilings, the radio falls suddenly silent and the heart stops; it is for those who have lived through this Prague night, lain awake in the darkness, to tell of it. That is why we have Milan Kundera and Václav Havel. Later, all will come to know what night this is. He who does not see the living Brezhnev may, who knows, see Ceausescu dead. There will be something for everyone to see.

She wants to see her train ticket, for the train leaves soon. She wants to see what seat number she has, and whether it is a lucky number or not. As she searches in her pocket for the ticket, her glance falls on an old, black mirror on the wall, like a piece of framed night-darkness. In the mirror are chairs, shelves, and the billiard-green sofa, covered in cushions. The room in the mirror shimmers as if it has just been born into empty space. The night-darkness throws a shadow over everything that exists. Her own face, too, feels naked and dangerous, as if its flesh and bone had been taken away. Now nothing protects this face, and from this face no one is protected.

She lowers her head, her neck is bared and on it falls a kiss, like the blade of a guillotine.

This sentence, written much later and by a completely different author, could appear on the floor at their feet at this moment, like the text of a silent movie; but she would not read it anyway, for now she stands with her eyes against his eyes and her teeth against his teeth, sees, close up, the skin of his face and his eyelashes, in speaking of which one cannot avoid the well-known old phrase, the sweet, sombre fairy-tale cliché: 'Ivory and blood. Ebony.' For a long breath they survey each other in a strange gaze, seeing one another only as substance and material, as meaning and sign, as line and form, as booty. A mutual, cold, furtive glance, which both understand at once and which forces them to take note; a glance that mixes with the blood-taste of a kiss, makes them for a moment playmates and comrades-in-arms.

Anyone who saw the expressions on their faces might quite easily think of the two water-sprites of the folk-tale who met at a village fair under the linden trees, having come there, without each others' knowledge, to seduce farmers' daughters and millers' sons.

The linden rustles, a flock of jets roars across Latvia's airspace, the train ticket is no longer necessary, it can be thrown away. She squeezes the hours that follow like a human heart, or black, red-fleshed berries. She presses them to a pulp and drinks the juice.

It is not irrelevant to mention here that a mark has been left on her being by Good Friday 1951, when darkness covered the earth, snow began to fall in large, wet flakes, the wagtail's feet froze to the ground and in the yard, in a tin tub, a great pike struggled with death; it was to be killed as soon as the child had been read the Bible story next to the picture of the burnt offering.

During the pauses while the pages were being turned, she could hear the fish flailing against the tub with its tail, and the desperate and sorrowful booming of the tub. The great fish's death throes and the ringing of the metal, snow, ice and reading aloud belong with her conception of love as surely as the commandment: 'Take fire, take a knife.' For that reason she resolves now, looking him in the eye: 'If I should have to bring Jehovah a burnt offering, I now know where I should find it. I should take *this one, here.*'

The room has grown dark. Brezhnev's tanks have just reached Prague. The Angel of the Lord smiles mockingly and tenderly. In his hand is no fiery sword, no lance, no spear or brine-soaked whip, but only a single stinging nettle, which gives strength to resist evil and purifies the blood.

Smoke rises vertically from factory chimneys, iron rumbles, bare bulbs light corridors and stairways. Do not trust others. It is better not to speak about yourself. Fear glows in naked forty-watt bulbs like an egg, like butter and cream, like an official testimony.

17

Clouds float like leaflets over the long lonely beaches of the Baltic, over tracks left by soldiers' boots and bloodhounds. Forests groan in Bohemia and Moravia, the wind bends the grain of Lithuania double, strikes the beans of Latvia to the ground. More faith! More hope! More love! You must not forget that under the cushion is a telephone which you cannot use until you have learnt the secret language. Whoever once understands it can never escape it, but becomes a participant in everything that happens. You must remember that on the telephone you cannot use the words 'book', 'papers', 'document', 'suitcase', 'letter', 'men'. A book may be banned, even printed abroad, papers are the same thing as a document, but a document can always be forged. A suitcase suggests things being moved from one place to another. But what kind of things? And where from? A letter can even be brought by hand across the border. Men may *dissent*, there is every reason to suppose they do. Men are always more suspect than women. For safety's sake, men must always be called by women's names, and Paris rechristened Kiev, New York Moscow. But 'at auntie's house' nevertheless means 'in Kiev', and 'at uncle's' means 'in Moscow'. It is not worth letting the names of Tallinn or Riga cross your lips unnecessarily. You can always talk about butter and eggs. It is highly recommended. You can talk about dogs, too, but not about muzzles, because muzzles provoke undue attention, and that is not necessary. About Aunt Olga, mother, the health centre, cabbage and beetroot you can talk as much as you like. Times mentioned should preferably be during the day, as evening is by its nature suspicious. Of the night it is better not to speak at all, Lord protect us from the night.

If you want to say, 'I'll come next Wednesday evening at eight', then say: 'Aunt Olga will send mother the eight black coat buttons she asked for next Wednesday'. Or eight and a half kilos of blackcurrants. Or seven jars of olives, black, not green. Or black plimsolls at six roubles. In any case, night is black. You have to learn to talk about Aunt Olga's life. You must never say 'telegram'; speak instead of 'a packet of butter'. You'll get the hang of it. Even a bear can be taught to dance. It's not worth

18

puzzling over everything. If you hear someone fretting, 'I haven't heard anything of Kuzminichna's son-in-law for a while, is he still involved in the art world?', it means that the emigration papers have got stuck somewhere again, and the official who was supposed to arrange the matter through contacts is on holiday, or on a business trip, or has been moved to a different department. Anyone who arranges things through *connections* is *Kuzminichna's son-in-law*, you must remember this and not show your surprise if he turns out to be not a man but a woman. He is a *son-in-law*, all the same. Kuzminichna herself exists; you take her Latvian honey and real cotton yarn, which mother buys at the market.

Of mother and Aunt Olga she knows today as yet very little. In the future she will understand even ordinary words wrongly for quite some time, and for that reason she will have about the family, which, as yet, she has not even seen, mysterious, wild imaginings which she will not divulge to anyone. She feels certain that Aunt Olga fishes for *perch* in the evenings, for it has been said in her hearing that in the evenings Aunt Olga's *arches* ache, and the similar ring of those words in a foreign language deceives her. The secret language makes the matter especially confusing. She can never understand whether the talk is simply of buying butter and cream or of the arrival of fateful news from OVIR.

The parquet clicks to itself. It is already too dark. Nothing can be seen. Perhaps whole decades rustle back and forth in the darkened room; but perhaps it is the draught that stirs the curtain. If it were not so dark all her vertebrae could be seen at this moment, each one separately. Even though they are invisible, he counts them all as if making a declaration or swearing an oath, with his bare hand and quite alone. Both his names, the secret Lion and the public Lev, his own tomorrow and even his grandfather's grave in New York, he delivers up at this moment with touching faith to the despotism of a smile and a gaze which, in the darkness, he cannot even see.

He cannot guess that those same fingers, whose bones he has today learned to know like his own five fingers, which he has shaped from clay and even remodelled twice, that at that moment those same fingers are writing in the air, in Estonian, above his shoulder-blade the Russian wishing charm, 'By the pike's command, by my will', and that the mouth he believes he already knows, which he has shaped anew so many times, that that mouth is smiling into the night's darkness as if human destiny and earthly sorrow were no more than mockery and banter.

The Angel of the Lord wrinkles his brow and comes closer. In the dead silence of the night, countries and people are moving from West to East, so that not even a dog barks.

2

In the sombre and sparkling light of late summer, fear flashes like a silver ear-trumpet into which one cannot speak, but only whisper and wheeze. TASS makes announcements, but nothing can be heard. In Stockholm and in Helsinki, in Hamburg and in Vienna there flashes across the evening news for perhaps a moment the image of a burnt offering – the strange and desperate protest of a longhair against the tanks, against the background of picturesque views of Prague and Brezhnev's forces. A Czech boy pouring petrol over himself and then lighting a match does not really go with the carpets in the living-room of Europe, so the television is switched off. An endless, eternal darkness may be seen in the yawner's mouth. A handful of grey dust falls over everything that exists.

After this, only large and extremely large buildings are constructed in Estonia, Latvia and Lithuania. A quite extraordinary size is demanded of barns and schools. From time to time smaller children get lost as they return from a distant large school, board the wrong bus and do not make it home for the night. Afterwards, they are unable to say where they spent the night. Perhaps in a cannibal's hut? Perhaps in the Tontla forest or the hell of Tori? The radio tells the story of a poor little seven-year-old who got lost in a neighbouring village as he looked for the road home; he did not dare ask anyone the way, and was found the following morning at the bus-stop, cold and stiff, his satchel faithfully on his back.

From now on all hedges are cut back from the sides of the roads, as fields must be open, while roads and rivers must be straight as an arrow. If they are not, they are straightened. The fate

21

of the songbird, the hedgehog and the hare is much discussed. No one tells anyone else what they really think.

The shores of lakes and rivers are built full of saunas. Some people, it is true, fall asleep on the boards and are roasted, but this does not frighten the others. In the evenings, people gather around the saunas and smoke-ovens, gnaw bones, drink spirits and beer and press them on small boys, rage and brawl. The empty bottles are smashed against the rocks. Gazes become greedy, expressions insolent.

Nevertheless, ready-written books stand unshaking on the shelves like a threat and a liberation, a promise or a secret assurance, although they have been burned in many fires by order of the State and chopped with many axes. As one raises one's gaze from these books, one can see with completely new eyes how the restless light of morning turns, as the day progresses, into the peaceful glimmer of evening. How the clouds arrive from the beginning of the century and fly again over Austria and Hungary, Riga and Tallinn, over world wars, illusions, irony and love, over fire and water, toward the end of the century. How the message sooner or later reaches its destination and how nothing has ended or will ever end. Everything happens at once, as always.

Brides dressed in white float through the boundless and infinite realm of Brezhnev like a band of travelling players blown by the wind. They set their dearly bought, expensive bridal bouquets on top of the tips of Lenin's boots, and before the dead statue their living white necks are helplessly and frighteningly bare.

The party leaders of the Eastern Bloc approach the statue with practised official steps, wearing dark blue summer coats, their gold teeth and the wash-proof silver of their temples glittering. On the tips of the boots of the deceased they set living roses bought with party funds, so fresh and red that it is as if a drop of blood has been poured on to their roots. The party leaders laugh and narrow their eyes in satisfaction. But isn't Dubček missing today? Where is Dubček? Perhaps TASS can tell us? The oracle of TASS answers, unasked: 'Dubček did not check the activities of revisionists or counter-socialist forces, but nevertheless the counter-revolutionary plans fostered by international imperialism have been annulled. The message of the party workers and important figures, the communists and workers of Czechoslovakia has been heard; the forces of brotherly countries have already arrived in Czechoslovakia.'

All of this remains beyond the horizon, and despite this news great summer clouds with glittering edges move in a long, festive line across the sky. If one looks at them for a while, one can easily forget what year it is; life is endlessly long, there is plenty of time and the road does not lead forward or backward, but directly upwards.

Today at noon the beaches are completely empty. None of the city's local trains go to so distant and lonely a place. Lion knows this beach well, for he has been here before, waiting and watching for some kind of sign. Like this, without any kind of sign, it is difficult to decide what to do. Should he really simply raise the curtain to the promised land and see with his own eyes what is behind it? What to do?!

Just a couple of weeks ago, Lion saw a rainbow on this beach, one end in a large willow-bush, just like the ladder in Jacob's dream. It rose from the bush and was like a spirit of seven colours. If only he knew whether it was a *sign* or just a *coincidence*. Lion claims passionately that he does not, in any case, believe in signs; he cannot believe because his reason forbids it. Then he would have to believe in all sorts of nonsense.

At the same time his eyes look mockingly through the words he has just uttered and see behind them the willow bush in which Jacob's ladder stands. To shatter the image, Lion grasps her hand and squeezes its bones and flesh with his own so hard against his eyes that all that is left is a black darkness in which there dances a red spark of flame.

The one and only shadow of the two of them falls on the wind- and bird-track-covered sand, on the lilac flowers of the sea shore, on the picture of the burnt offering with its threateningly flickering distance, on silence and whiteness. An unfounded joy strikes them on the head like a flame.

On either side, the long sand beaches disappear beyond the curvature of the earth. Below, they become the beaches of Lithuania, Poland and the two Germanies. These shores begin at Saulkrast, but they are not in the habit of ending at Travemünde. Above, there is nothing but Estonia – a white and empty sky, cows up to their bellies in water, the sparse, salt grass of the shore meadows and the callous whistling of the wind. Farther up it is impossible to go – there are water and weapons.

On the dunes grow willows. Their red-barked branches glow threatening and austere. In spring and autumn they are seared by the ice-cold tides. Thus in the end all that is left of them are white, salty skeletons. The sand carries the smell of hot pencils that have been in the sun for a long time and dry, yellow paper. Solitary bees find their way here from the heathlands and seek their way back. Although the sky is as deep and blue as an altar painting, a warning line of haze remains on the skyline. The sound of the sand under bare feet is as sharp as the swish of a wing.

The buzzing of bees, the flash of swallows. The phantom-like hours, running through the fingers, time in its brilliance, without past and without future. The honeyed scent of a strange plant and the scent of blood through the skin.

They sat on an electric train for an hour and a half, made their way at random through the dry, crackling pine forest, entangled themselves in the young spruce thicket and rejoiced on seeing the sea. She stalked Lion, who walks ahead, from behind his back with an experienced stalker's gaze, kept him in sight like an open book, the face of a clock or a half-open oven.

She has noticed that the forest flowers, the pine trees and the mossy glades pay not the slightest attention to Lion. He does not merge with them or disappear, but catches the eye in an extraordinary way, like a bookshelf on the forest floor. His way of being in the forest is somehow ill-omened and exciting, just like the bookshelf's existence in the forest. As if it were connected with confused things, escape and concealment. Particularly exciting is Lion's back. Here it is much lonelier and older than it was in the city. As she observes him she finds in the thicket a striped feather.

She feels that it must be the feather only of a cuckoo or a buzzard, but not of an innocent songbird. With this cuckoo feather she touches his back so secretly that he does not even notice. Thus Lion never knows that behind his back there has occurred a serious attempt to promise faithfulness and to declare love.

Then they have reached the sea shore, near the bush where the foot of Jacob's ladder was. Here on the sea shore something has happened to them, something which until now, with indifferent and ignorant eyes, they have only read about in books – time itself has revealed itself to them, has given them a sign of its nature and its power.

They are those who change and move; time does not move in the way they believe it does, but completely differently. What they consider to be the movement of time is nothing more than their own youth, nothing more than their own age, nothing more than their own mortality; over it a white bird flies, the smell of seaweed and water rises, the wind blows. Not in Prague or even Moscow is everything lost as long as the living wind blows and the sky shows its colours.

They know nothing of Prague, and Moscow does not interest them in the slightest. Their day rests on the long beach like a gift from an idol with a sly smile. They break off glittering moments and throw them carelessly over one another's shoulders. But they have enough sense in their heads to keep quiet, otherwise all that would be heard from their mouths would be very well-worn words.

They have finally made a fire between the dunes, for it is as if the dry branches of the dead willows were made for fire-making. The flame has no colour; it is transparent, and it is as if there were no fire on the sand, but only the illusion of fire. What they leave unsaid is said by the flame. Is said by the red and white skeletons of the willow bushes and by the white line that is drawn in the sky over the sea by the military aeroplane.

There is no telephone here, and *no need for a secret language.* Here things can be called by their real names, if they have them. The feather of which they do not know whether it belonged to a cuckoo or a buzzard is thrown, with a single movement of the hand, into the fire and burns away without anyone ever hearing its real name. Everything the eye sees has only a temporary, mutually agreed name. What exactly, depends on language. Perhaps only the Angel of the Lord knows the real names, on hearing which even the sand and the lifeless stone can begin to move, but at this moment the Angel of the Lord has turned his back and washed his hands. His calves gleam as he wades into the sea.

Smoke rises from the fire, the shadows strengthen; the time of silence is over. Lion leans up on his elbows; his shoulders are tanned and shine like polished wood – as if he had hewn his own shoulders, without the help of Jehovah, free of the flesh of the world, and rubbed them until they shone, with his own hands. As the light falls toward evening, the colour of his eyes is clearly visible – it is not brown or black, as one might earlier have supposed, but deep yellow, with a reddish glow, the colour of bees.

Now Lion speaks for a long time, with great sympathy, using a large number of words that are completely incomprehensible and unfamiliar to her. But he keeps returning to just one declaration: *'There is no country that is so precious that its earth should be carried in a bag at one's breast.'*

She to whom this challenge is directed should be able to accept it, to overturn it and throw it away; she should give him peace and comfort, but instead she is suspiciously quiet and draws masks and grimaces in the sand. She is completely at peace with herself; a small smile lifts the corners of her mouth. She can see with her own eyes and hear with her own ears that he trusts her. In fact she does not really hear what he is talking about. Her gentle smile conceals a number of things that would be surprising even to herself.

In fact at this moment she would like to be him, this Lion, the colour of whose eyes and the even tan of whose shoulders she follows with shameless and lustrous, larcenous looks. She is like a cuckoo or a crow who covets another's only nest and dearest possessions – nothing more and nothing less than his body and soul. If only it were in her power, she would, on this hot sand, in the midst of the bright day, amid the thunder of the aeroplanes and the regular, recurrent rumble of the electric trains, snatch his spirit, grossly and crudely, from his nostrils and breathe her own spirit into its place.

It has to be said that, kiss by kiss, she grows a little closer to her goal. She feels as if he has already been born at her order, precisely here and at precisely this moment. But nevertheless, the word 'earth' in his mouth makes her cautious and returns her from the kingdom of suspicious daydreams to living life, in which the most secret of thoughts are hidden, in which everything happens in a regulated way and in which one may not omit a single heartbeat or a single moment.

Privately, she is amazed at the fact that Lion uses such old-fashioned words as 'bag' and 'earth'. Especially earth. It brings to her mind kerchiefed old ladies in their aprons, complaining, 'What does it matter about me, earth to earth,' or 'I don't know if my old bones will even be good enough for the earth of the graveyard.'

About earth she knows a thing or two. She never mixes light, brown, sandy earth with the heavy, red earth of the claypit; she has seen how earthworms, potatoes and root vegetables, rusty penknives, buttons, boot-legs, spruce-stumps and the jawbones of animals emerge from the earth. She has gazed into the bottom of an opened grave and seen there the marks of body and spade. The threat, 'From earth did you come and to earth you shall return,' makes earth her blood-enemy, with which she has accounts to settle.

A light and warm wind blows straight from the open sea, changes direction and raises sparks high from the fire. As they fall, the living red sparks become grey flecks of dust. Lion brings one more armful of dry willow-branches to the fire, and they crackle noisily. He also brings white reeds that have been washed up on the shore; as they burn, they scatter embers in every direction. Air, water and fire have, as evening falls, become restless and begun to move.

27

The restlessness of his surroundings also clings to Lion; he no longer stays still, but sits and rises, seeks a new and better place for himself, turns his back to the sea and asks of everything he has just seen – of the stones and of the waters, of the fir-trees and of the willows – and of everything that cannot be seen – of the darkness, which the horizon can still at this moment conceal, of the old borders of the realm that have sunk beneath the earth's surface, of the White Sea and the Black Sea, asks of Brezhnev himself and separately of the leader of every Soviet republic – why must he bow to states simply because he has a state passport in his pocket? Why must he *kiss the earth* here, when his *graves* are elsewhere?

The bookish words, 'kiss the earth' and 'graves' became, in his mouth, as prosaic and everyday as the words 'station' or 'housing co-operative board'. As he speaks, the tone of Lion's voice becomes judgmental and his face darkens. He freezes to the spot, and it is as if his shoulders are covered in dust. He is afraid that he will receive a *negative* response from OVIR, that Kuzminitchna's *son-in-law* has been given other responsibilities and that he no longer looks after artistic matters. But what does looking after artistic matters mean in the secret language? Of course, arranging emigrations.

He now fears a *positive* response still more than a *negative* one. He fears it, even though he made his decision to leave so long ago that he no longer remembers when. Perhaps it was when they still had a dog called Nosson, which ate all the cigarette stubs it could find on the ground. This must have been in second or third form, because in the autumn of fourth form Nosson set off after the cigarette-smokers and down-and-outs and never came home. He was lolling in front of the beer-bar when Aunt Olga saw him once, but Nosson looked through her, kept his nerve, and pretended not to recognise her.

It is from those times that the preparation for departure begins, for the disappearance of Nosson-the-dog was a sure sign: now it is time to get going, it is not worth waiting. Even Nosson is no longer an obstacle; there is no need to wonder how long the dog has left to live. Preparation for departure has taken so long that they have got a new dog, Kinski, and he already has frost in his beard.

For Lion, preparations for departure have meant the sacrifice of Tuesday evenings to the German language and the sacrifice of Thursday evenings to the English language. The secret language and telephone etiquette he learned when he learned to speak, through play. Aunt Olga has telephoned him often and always asked for Lev, and he has answered promptly and firmly, 'Lev here'. Himself, he does not even yet understand why it should be Lev, when his *passport* says Lion. Nevertheless Lion is certain that where he has not had to show his passport, it has been useful to him. Especially at school.

Here, in front of the fire, he also confesses that he has made two bronze milkmaids and one head of Lenin of *local* stone, and that he has been ashamed of them ever since. The head of Lenin won him a prize in Moscow. He sees the head in his dreams, and always in the same way – he is hurrying along the corridor at OVIR and behind him toddles Lenin's head, without a body, low, smooth and black, like a dog. He tries to hide the head in the hem of his coat, badly afraid that Kuzminitchna will see it and be displeased and let it be known that her son-in-law no longer looks after artistic matters.

As he relates this, an extraordinary, sombre, expression of joy lights up Lion's eyes. He describes his old, fleecy American coat and its hemline, which was long just at the time when short coats were worn in Brezhnev's Kingdom. He illustrates history correctly with pictures and draws Kuzminitchna's outline in the sand. He takes particular care with her earrings and spectacle frames. The sand is dry and falls back into the grooves, but Lion crawls along the shore, wipes a few lines away and draws more in their place, until Kuzminitchna's face begins to resemble Beethoven's death-mask.

Both of them, the drawer and the watcher, are now lolling around on the sand, laughing, and their lightheartedness is frankly astonishing. It feels as if no kingdom could prevent their eyes from shining or their teeth from gleaming. They do not turn hot or

29

cold on account of the destinies of thousands of political prisoners or because of the secrets of the mental hospitals. What do they care about other people! What of it that the earth around them is cursed! After all, no one who has been here under the shelter of Intourist's warm wing believes that. This is *a land of dreams, where a book costs as little as a loaf of bread, where apartment rents are unusually low, where attention is not paid merely to external appearances, where fear of tomorrow is unknown.*

They draw Kuzminitchna's portrait at the edge of the giant Kingdom, on the strip of earth at its extremity, and pay no heed to the cities that howl behind their backs or to the filing cabinets in which their names may appear noted down at any moment. The Angel of the Lord does not, after all, grasp a large pair of scissors or cut their laughter short; it dies down in its own time. The years they have not yet lived fall straight down from above, from the middle of the sky; the shadow of parting covers their faces like a black tent, the flame freezes to the spot and the wind does not blow. Then the sky closes again, the shadow is rolled up and pulled back, the smoke begins to circle around itself on the spot. Everything is as it was.

Lion says he does not know whether he is living in a *strange country* at this moment or whether he will begin to live in a *strange country* in the future, and she answers, profoundly, that he will not know this until the future arrives. From Lion's mouth she leans that it is possible to leave the Kingdom. Unbelievable, but to her this thought is entirely new. It agitates her so much that she scratches the horsefly bites on the skin of her slender, gleaming ankle-bones until they bleed.

Her head is full of details of pictures from colour magazines, rubbish which she secretly, ashamed and lustful, allows to come into view from the labyrinthine corridors of her own memory. Forced to choose between a serious novel and a cheap illustrated magazine, she has chosen both. Above Vienna she has seen a woman hovering, with a bra whose name is Triumph. Isolde she has seen pouring advertising coffee into Tristan's cup. In a quiet pool in the Imatra river swims the swan of Tuonela, in its beak a life-insurance document. Ecstatic choirs sing: 'Dior! Mercedes! Volvo! Braun! Dior! Mercedes! Volvo! Braun!' Car keys, diamond rings and beer cans drift everywhere. The teeth of adult men are white and their necks red. Lion ought to take the existence of these men seriously and think about it, but instead he tells her the life story of Warhol, describes the sculptures of Henry Moore and confesses what he has been told about American light. 'There, the light is yellow. There, the shadows are yellow. Don't make the mistake of supposing they're blue,' he warns. He says he thinks about Moore's sculptures all the time, and that he is bothered above all by these sculptures' shadows. 'Their shadows work. They work to the benefit of the sculptures.' He confesses that he has also followed the shadows of his own sculptures; if there is something wrong with them, they do not *work*. 'When the shadow lives, the sculpture is ready,' he reveals his professionalism to her.

As he speaks, he examines the shadows of himself and her on the sand; his gaze becomes absent and his hands sink humbly to his sides, for they have been given too difficult a task – they must make of a living body a dead statue whose shadow is nevertheless alive. He cannot forgive her for the fact that she moves, changes her expressions, lives and changes. For the face, after all, Lion has selected the correct expression; he has bent the vertebrae of the neck to a suitable angle with his own hands, and there they should stay. They should reveal the hand that touched them and the gaze that made them live. Only as such will they finally belong to that hand and that gaze.

Lion sets his hand on her neck just as if he really did want to bend it, and their shadows merge once more. Not a single word can describe the burning sorrow they feel together, since neither of them can escape the limit set to mortals, which shelters the being of one from the other. If that limit were not set, they would at once exchange their bones and their flesh as if they were the clothes they wear. They would conquer the strange blood-darkness, take up proprietorial rights in one another's skull; one would take the other's lungs, would squeeze their damp and raw

31

darkness together, would try on the other's kidneys and heart, would pull the other's spine straight like a bright and terrifying spring. Feeling curiosity and dread, one would sense the other doing exactly the same in their own flesh.

The air is as damp as the salt of tears. The wind changes direction. Lion remains standing alone in the bright sunlight while she shakes her hands from his neck and sets out for the water, her back straight, her head up. In his spirit Lion sees her complete, a yellow-brown wooden sculpture. The only thing of which he is not quite sure is the wood of which the sculpture is made. Birch and pearwood he dismisses immediately. When he reaches walnut, he is certain. At that very moment the other looks over her shoulder and on her face he sees a naked and bare joy which makes her as innocent and cruel as daylight, as liberated from the power of time as the grass which disappears in October and reappears in May, as unreachable as the horizon. Each of her footprints tears the sand open.

She pauses next to a solitary dewberry bush and eats all its berries, every last one of them. The dark red juice flows along her fingers and she wipes her hands carelessly clean against her stomach. One thing is certain – she can never make this movement again. Never again will she be so young. Never again, and from eternity to eternity. So full of pathos is the signature to this painting, it has only a strip of sand, sea-water and human destiny, that of those who are alive today.

She allows the sea-water to rise to her breast; only then does she begin to swim. The water does not ripple, not a wave splashes; all around is silence and emptiness, as if a door had closed behind her back.

It is worth remembering that the person who is swimming here is the same child who, in 1956, walks along a green forest path, on her face the classic patches of summer sun and the old, poetic pattern of leaves. Under her arm she carries a thick book whose name is *The Russian Forest*. She believes it is her responsibility to read it from cover to cover, since she has borrowed it from the library. She intends to climb up a bird-cherry tree, eat berries and read her book. Bluebells glow on either side of the forest path as if in vases on an altar. A dark scent of resin rises from the spruces, and along the path walks the small son of the director of the collective farm, who has been given a simple task – to see whether the raspberries of the forest are ripe.

The boy may be five or six years old. In his hand he has a rubber rooster that whistles. The path winds between the raspberry canes and brings the children inevitably closer. They stop, scrape the ground with their feet, fiddle with their buttons and pick berries from the bushes. The collective director's son is at least five years younger than her and looks even smaller, although when he grows up he will be as sturdy as a wild bull.

The leaf-shadows that move over the face of the bigger child give her a clever and intriguing expression; she takes measure of the hesitant little boy from head to toe and tempts him: 'Come with me, I'll show you a secret place.' When the other does not know how to reply and makes no move, the bigger child forces him: 'Well,' she says, wrinkling her eyebrows. A black ray sparkles in her bright eyes. And look – the boy slips obediently after her into the thick spruce thicket, where one must be careful not to poke one's eyes out of one's head.

After a little while, the older child pushes the younger one through the thick spruce branches into the sunlight, which beats straight down from above, into a small clearing in the forest. The smell of cut hay fills the whole glowing and shimmering airspace. Butterflies disappear from light into shade and unexpectedly become visible again. Where the shadow falls, the earth is as black as the mouth of hell. The trees murmur barely audibly. Everyone has seen that clearing; countless paintings have been made of it, and it has been described in various languages. It is that very same clearing. The boy stands still, a disappointed expression on his face; he cannot see anything in particular in the clearing and is ready at once to begin whining; he squeaks his rubber cockerel crossly.

And he would not have been at all afraid if the other had not whispered: 'Fear not. I am here,' at the same time gradually

33

pushing the little one forward, into the middle of the bright light. Now the entire glistening and rustling clearing is full of whispering: 'Fear not. As long as I am here, *it will not come.*'

Then a branch breaks, the bushes close like a secret door and the whisperer has disappeared from the clearing. Holding her breath, she creeps to the other side of the clearing and peeps through the branches. In the midst of the parade-ground brilliance and lustre of the July day stands a small, grey figure who does not even dare whimper. He merely presses his yellow rubber rooster with both hands against his neck. Later, at home, the lost boy, who has been found with great difficulty, is unable to say anything intelligible.

Twenty years later, a certain man wipes this clearing and its bushes off the face of the earth with a bellowing caterpillar truck. Then this man is paid a wage and awarded a prize. If only it were in his power, he would never let the sun shine here.

It may be that seven hundred years of slavery, ghosts, water-spirits and earth-spirits are merely the imagination of the Estonian nation and an object of folkloristic study; but it may be that every Estonian tractor-driver knows what they are.

Whether Lion has something to do with this story or not will become clear only in the future . At this moment, however, Lion is carrying sand to the campfire until the flame is suffocated; then he stands on the grave of the fire, his arms crossed on his chest. No one can know what he is thinking. He follows with interest how she gradually retrieves her limbs from the sea and how they take on their former shape once again. Shoulders are shoulders again, and knees are knees, not an indefinite vibration under the water. Her lips are blue from the long rinsing in the sea and her skin is in goosepimples. As soon as she sets foot on the shore, she steps on a broken light-bulb which the waves have found somewhere and brought with them. The thin glass cuts her soft skin easily and without causing particular pain.

Naturally she leans her arm on Lion's shoulder and examines the sole of her foot, standing on her other leg. Then she sits down on the sand and orders: 'Take a knife.' It is such a simple sentence that everyone ought to be able to say it in a foreign language. Without saying a word, Lion takes the wet, sandy foot under his arm, and with a single, skilful movement his valuable Swiss penknife lifts the piece of glass out of the wound. The narrow streak of blood which makes its appearance is not worth mentioning. Nevertheless, it glistens in the evening light like a cheap ornament. Lion takes possession of it. Blood has the taste of blood, whoever it belongs to.

Whose are Brezhnev's tanks? Whose are the sorrow of the western sky and the poison of books? And whose are '*the pair of lovers who fearlessly run along the shore, barefoot, barefoot, intoxicated by the wind...*'.

Today TASS no longer announces anything. On the shores of both the river Daugava and the Gulf of Finland, water flows from taps into saucepans and coffee pots, bathtubs and wash-hand basins. Butter is taken out of refrigerators, bread is cut.

The sun god hurries toward the West, straight through the Iron Curtain without blinking. Its bare fiery knees glitter above attempted coups and missile bases as unwaveringly as they glitter above apple-tree branches and rose-hips that have been put out to dry. And as the law decrees, its chariot always sets out from the Red Square in Moscow an hour earlier than from the Riga shore.

3

White plates appear on the table, and are cleared away again. The breadknife is forgotten, and is not put back in its place. Coffee grounds and tea leaves are thrown away. The windows are open to the August evening. The curtain flutters so innocently, the bunch of flowers in the vase smells so sweet and the circle of light thrown by the ceiling lamp glows so warmly that it feels as if down in Prague it could not, after all, already be autumn and as if up here in Riga the State could not set its hand on human days and as if the work of the officers of staff of the Baltic military district were mere imagination or mockery.

Everyone who puts his head out of the window draws it back quickly, for the night is as large and dark as the kingdom of death. On the other side of the window stands the Angel of the Lord, notebook in hand, writing. What he notes for today he keeps to himself, as he does everything he sees as he looks through house walls and ribs. Nevertheless, there are two words – *smoke* and *salt* – which he must set down for today, for in his opinion the entire state is nothing but blue smoke which was and which no longer is, and human days and bodies are, according to him, only salt, which dissolves. One could argue with him, and with him arguments have truly been held. Is a human being an animal? Attempts could be made, with the help of books, to explain this to him, and this really has been explained, but he does not even bother to raise his eyebrows. Arguing with him is like carrying water in a sieve.

The first stars are appearing in the sky. Certainly there will be some among them that fall into the nettles of Estonia, the flowers of Latvia and the mud and dust of the Czechs.

As if what is happening today beyond the horizon did not

concern them at all, Lion opens cupboard doors and linen chests and pulls out, as if from the maw of a wild beast, bathtowels and cloths. Before the fresh piles of clothes and the scented bags with drawstring necks, made with care and love, she feels a distinct confusion and embarrassment. It is not known when the mythical mother or Aunt Olga will make their appearance. All that is known is that they are sitting in the villa; and with his father, at that. His father has not been mentioned earlier. This is the first time his father enters the game.

But in the name of honesty there has not been talk of many matters, such as now, for example, of her flat in Tallinn, where only cold water issues from the taps and where life is played at and acted out rather than really lived. There has been no talk of hand-towels and bedlinen which have been put in the oven because someone has wiped paint on them from a paintbrush; nor of shabby clothes or records that are constantly circulated and exchanged. In particular, there has been no talk of the fact that no one has brothers or sisters, a mother or a father. Relatives are not spoken about. Mother and Father? What kind of creatures are they?

Because she has not for a long time been in places where jam is boiled, chops are fried or bedclothes are ironed, she is certain that boiling, frying and ironing have been abandoned, everywhere and in general. Now she sees on the table cherry sauce made by Aunt Olga and in the linen cupboard sheets ironed by Mother, and it is a considerable blow to her. In her heart she wonders greatly at the sauce and the sheets, just as she wonders at the fact that Lion uses them without a care, as if he had heard nothing of the musical *Hair* or of the future of the world. In any case, she is very impressed by the big cherry-sauce jar. So nothing has changed! The jam-jars are always in the cupboard and everywhere is neat and tidy! Why then all those midnight trips, the flower on the back of the shirt, words and colour and the fate of the world! Why then have bridges been burned, fathers' footholds been gnawed away and mothers' potato salads despised!

What does she expect as she stretches out her hand and sets it on the lifeline of his hand? For a moment they stand facing one another outside the bathroom door, hand in hand, like ambassadors whose kingdoms have, against all expectation, entered an alliance, even if it is not yet known to what purpose. All that is missing is for them to assure one another, with frank gazes and clear, official smiles, 'Good luck. Strength and success!' But perhaps they should instead whisper to one another, demandingly: 'Fear not! I am here!'

From the bottom of her heart she hopes that Lion will tear apart all her nets and ropes, throw them over his shoulder and nevertheless stay with her; will understand her, see through her and comfort her. But how could Lion do so, when he himself, not three years ago, smiled a charming smile, coldly calculating, at his teacher and at the director of his diploma project. When he caught in his net a frightening and large fish, followed its thrashing for some time feeling sombre curiosity and fear, and left it gasping air at a suitable moment. In any case, Lion defended his diploma project brilliantly, and everyone present remembers to this day the boy's frank gaze. She is not sure what Lion guesses about her, and what the State knows. No one can help her.

Then the long, arrow-shaped hands of the wall-clock click, time moves itself and it feels as if its bones were creaking. The clock strikes, and the harmonious, clear, woman's voice of the strokes echoes through the apartment like a sign that one must live and work as long as life lasts.

Lion pushes the cupboard doors shut and offers her a carefully folded bathtowel which she places carelessly on her shoulder. She locks the frosted glass door of the strange bathroom with a confident hand, turns on the taps and scatters her few clothes carelessly across the floor. The towel has the old-fashioned smell of snow and lavender of *painfully* clean new clothes, but even this she crumples up into a heap and throws on to the floor, despite the fact that there is a whole row of empty hooks on the wall.

She sizes up the bathroom. In her opinion, it is a bathroom for old people. This is indicated, in particular, by the feet on the bathtub, which are cast in iron although they attempt to look like brass. The paint on the white chair is worn, and wooden lilies curl limply on the mirror frame, and even they bring to her mind old people and second-hand shops, but not the art nouveau pages of design magazines.

With the vigilant gaze of a hunter, she inspects her surroundings, not ignoring a single jar, bottle or box. Everything that shines, in particular, tempts her. As one might guess. She shifts scissors, tweezers and razor blades from one place to another and enjoys their damned and dangerous readiness for absolutely anything. Carelessly she adds to the phrase, 'alone in a strange bathroom', peculiar details. Where many visitors to strange bathrooms sniff at other people's perfumed soaps and deodorants, she discovers a cylindrical stone jar in which stand three strange toothbrushes – one white as bone, the second red as a mouth, the third black as ebony. Reddish brown veins wind through the white stone. It is unclear whether the stone is more reminiscent of the white knees of ancient gods or of the cold flesh and brown seeds of a bright summer apple.

She holds the stone in her hand until it grows warm, then puts it back on the shelf. Three toothbrushes and a tube of cheap Latvian peppermint toothpaste remain lying in the washbasin after her.

Without permission, she opens the cupboard under the mirror and looks thoroughly for shampoo, but does not find it until she has ransacked the whole cupboard. And although she finally finds a small cushion of egg shampoo, she throws it disparagingly back into the cupboard. A long-handled hand-mirror has emerged from the cupboard, beautiful but dim. And a shoebox filled with sticking plasters, pieces of amber, a pumice stone and a couple of blunt pencils. On to the floor roll tablets, acorns and pine-cones, and a considerable collection of angular stoppers from old perfume bottles, which the small Lion once considered his most precious treasures.

She stuffs all the things any old how back into the cupboard, pushes the door forcibly shut, and finally reaches the stage where she can step into the bath and turn on the shower. At the same

40

moment she is surrounded on every side by straight, thin and dense rods of water, like the bars of a cage. She stands naked in the cage, her head tipped back. The question naturally arises of where she came from and who let her in. Particularly when, as she steps out of the bath, she applies to her wet back other people's expensive and rare eye-cream. This she also rubs generously into the soles of her feet.

One drawer, however, has remained unexamined. And there she finds a dark red flannel bag and immediately pulls open its drawstring, leaving on the soft fabric greasy marks that smell of lotion. From the blackish-red mouth of the bag there crawls forth a sturdy, brown plait of hair, tightly bound at both ends with ordinary, cheap sewing thread.

It is not dusty and does not smell of old perfumes or naphtha, as one might imagine from its appearance; it has the ordinary smell of newly washed hair. When it touches the skin, it is like ordinary strange hair is – at the same time cold and warm, smooth and rough, repellent and alluring. One feels like passing it time and again through one's hands.

And that is exactly what she does, unknowing that this is *Mother's* schoolgirl plait, cut off where else but in Warsaw. More accurately, in 1932 in a certain Warsaw hairdresser's where Ada made quite *incomparable* water-curls for Grandmother. For her birthday, Mother was given a holiday in Warsaw and a haircut which, in her strict girl's school in Warsaw, had to be combed straight immediately and grown out. This cut-off plait then remained ungiven to Grandfather to take with him. It was supposed to be put in Grandfather's coffin when Grandfather died. In 1952 no one dared to go and ask the State for permission to leave the country for a funeral. Playing with this plait is not allowed.

No one can forbid her to play with it, for from now on the end of the plait is always in her hand. From now on, at any moment, she can look at the world through this young, soft, brown hair, which was not placed in the coffin, as she is doing just now. She does not herself know when and where she will allow this plait of hair to crawl forth from the bottom of her memory. She is as unpredictable and frightening as the future itself.

Although the spruce forests of Estonia, the vistas of Tallinn and the frosted glass door of the Latvian bathroom are behind her back, a hot, blue sky already undulates before her eyes, and a harsh, ominous wind blows along the broad Marszatkowska and along the lost Krochmalna – along all those streets which, it is true, bear the well-known names of Warsaw streets but which have remained inside and beneath the new, harsh and desperate Eastern Bloc Warsaw. As Warsaw streets, they exist only in the memory. With the help of memory anyone at all, for example Isaac Bashevis Singer, can allow Warsaw to rise as it was from the dead, to open the doors of apartments and cafés, which have not become ash and dust, to fill rooms with heartbeats and destinies. To allow, in half a page, a Warsaw winter's day to disappear, with the accompaniment of a quotation from Nietzsche, irrevocably and sadly; to summon up on to the walls an evening light, long gone, on to the radio a speech by Hitler and behind the glowing signs of the zodiac the mocking face of the strong Jehovah.

But memory in poetry, memory in prose and memory in drama are all different from memory in the chaos of life. They have no place for the humiliations of life, known to everyone and hidden from others: coffee does not spill on to clean shirt-fronts, shoes do not rub, a person rushing to a fateful meeting is not suddenly overtaken by an unexpected need to go to the lavatory or a feared fit of coughing. Hands never sweat, and it is always immediately clear why something happens.

And despite this, the glowing dotted line of memory passes through any darkness, the past announces itself in the future and the future in the past. As ye sow, so shall ye reap. In heaven as on earth. Since the year 1968 has passed, the year 1971 will inevitably come and the summer asphalt will melt, the road-surface will glow and Estonian tourists will hurry to the Warsaw shops. Solidarnosc and Walesa do not yet, as words, mean anything to anyone, but their seeds have been sown, and the time for harvest will come. Now, the Estonian tourists rummage eagerly through the Polish goods, although to them, too, they seem more expensive and of poorer quality than they imagined at home.

She is among the others, examining, like them, shoes and gloves, mentally counting her money. Like the others, she simply cannot decide what to buy. The end of the working day is approaching; the shops will close soon. Fluorescent lamps are burning in the shops, it is true, but nevertheless it feels as if electricity is being saved. The glowing heat of the streets cannot be felt at all inside. Inside, it is sweltering and dark. The old-fashioned smells of mould and iodoform spread in a remarkable way through these new buildings. The lamps chirrup and hum, the light flickers.

The old, stunted shop assistants are like ghosts; they have penetrating gazes and yellowing lace collars. They are covered either in hoarfrost or in dust. From time to time they move from behind one counter to behind another and hiss. The shoe department is the object of their special surveillance.

Although shoes for women, men and children, as well as babies' slippers, are on show in the glass cabinets, the Estonians are enthusiastically searching for expensive winter boots in smooth leather for their wives, brides and daughters, but they cannot find exactly what they want. Apparently it is not yet the boot season, and on this account they are very angry with the Polish nation. They really begin to complain. Won't forgive them. Bring up the issue, right there by the shop counter, of the Schlachta's crimes.* But high in the darkness of the shelves, they are continually stalked by the cruelly priced party shoes, like bloodthirsty beasts.

Patent leather glitters and splatters light, but suede, on the other hand, absorbs it. The skin-coloured leather lining glows evenly; the gold letters of the factory markings recall the inscriptions on tombstones. With these hoof-like shoes on her feet, a woman can be completely satisfied with herself – her feet, too, are now the same as those of the devil, as fashion demands.

Next door stand the suitcases and briefcases, trailing belts and straps, hanging shoulder straps, whiplashes and muzzles. It would not be worth listing them if it were not for the fact that the Estonians, and she among them, are now seeing so many of them together for the very first time. Their own country must be poor indeed if even hard-soled Polish shoes and rough suitcases provide them with a vision of brilliance and luxury!

Under the counter glass lie the gloves. Gloves arranged in fan shapes and carelessly thrown down, as if taken from an invisible hand. In this sweltering store, inhabited by ghosts, it is a surprise to see gloves, which are waved with at railway stations and airports, which are left behind in cafés and taxis – worn-out, sentimental, timeless gloves from behind the Iron Curtain, gloves of yesterday's world.

Even back on the street, she is in the sway of the gloves for some time. Their scent accompanies her to the first street corner.

Outside, everything is different from before. The sun is just beginning to set; the sky is like pure flame and smoke. Old men emerge from gateways, staring insolently. The tramlines glow red, people and buildings seem ghostlike. The others who have been to Warsaw must know, better than she, the Belvedere castle, the squares and fountains of the restored old city, the Church of the Holy Cross, the urn containing Chopin's heart. But it may be questioned whether they have experienced the coming of dusk. No one has said anything about that.

The story has been told of two Polish artists who were as talented as children but as irritable as dogs. The story has been told of how the Poles stoned the car of a well-known Estonian writer which had Soviet register plates. When the writer became angry and got out of the car, the Poles cried, 'Oh, it's you, dear sir; we were already thinking, the devil knows who it is!' Someone had found a bunch of money in a Warsaw graveyard. Condoms with holes in them had been bought for children in the belief that they were American chewing gum. Some had seen the theatre director Grotowski, others Olbrychski, the film-star.

She is able to see very little compared to the others. Because she stretches out her hand in Riga in 1968 so frivolously to take a strange plait of hair, she must see many other places, among them Warsaw in 1971, through the hair which was never placed in the coffin at their Great Parting. The brown melancholy of this hair, that of an old photograph, sets its mark on everything that exists. On the air, the window-glass, ridiculous and immortal love, the white faces of strange people, the politics of Brezhnev and Johnson, cinema posters, her own striped T-shirt, which really ought to be washed today. If it does not dry in time for tomorrow, it can easily, if the weather is warm, be put on while still damp.

Just as she has made a decision regarding the shirt and is intending to cross the road, the invisible emerges from the shadow of the visible and everyone who intended to cross the road leaps back. The tram brakes so suddenly that the rails strike fire. From above, a gust of wind presses the wings of the Angel of Death, as it dashes downward, together like sheets of lead. People's hair rises upright on their heads, pieces of paper and rubbish fly into the air; in the darkness it is impossible to make out whether someone is pushing his own bicycle whose red glass cat's eye glows strongly, or whether a red fireball is moving through the air.

At first she thinks everyone is following the fireball, but then she notices that between the tramlines, on the ground, lies something which everyone wants to see. Then a tarpaulin is thrown over its head. The Angel of Death is already departing, but the police and the doctors are only just arriving. Yellow tablets are forced into the mouth of the tram-driver. The driver's eyes roll upward and he snorts as, with the help of two men, the doctors open his jaws.

But, looking over her shoulder, she creeps away, and no one stops her. Even though she was standing close to the accident, she does not know whether a bicycle was seen, or ball lightning. No one knows what happened.

An accidental witness appears in a completely different place, begins to speak much later, speaks of Gorbachev and thinks of Lenin, confuses the end with the beginning and repeats words which everyone has heard already, raves about the past and the future, oblivion and laughter.

45

But now it is high time to return to the year 1968 and to ask whether she is still running strange hair through her hands or whether she has already got dressed, perhaps even dried the bathroom floor. She should act more quickly, as there is not nearly as much time as she thinks. Her bare feet leave shiny face-cream marks on the floor, it will take a lot of effort before they are completely erased.

Looking at herself in the mirror interests her greatly, and she passes the time in this activity just as if she were a primitive person, a child or dear old Narcissus. But now she is particularly taken with her hot, blushing face and the pupils of her eyes which, in the weak light of the bathroom, look black. It must simply be hoped that the charming roses of her skin and the black grapes of her eyes will not last long once she has left the bathroom and that she will get the bronze and steel of her usual colouring back more quickly than is generally supposed, as all the windows are open and the chilly air is moving through the rooms.

When she finally steps out of the bathroom, the apartment is dark and empty, as if many years had passed. The glass beads in the ceiling lamps tinkle, and with the draught the tinkling passes through the entire apartment like a wave. All the lamps have been turned off; only the television, which she did not notice earlier, illuminates the empty room, whose cupboards and shelves are able to participate in the life of the State. Their smooth backs reflect magical images – meetings of administrative district committees, collective acts of worker heroism and the progress of the army. Even the cups in the crockery cupboard are unable to remain separate from living life, as *continual applause* makes everything in the cupboard rattle.

She has already understood a thing or two and put them behind her ear, and she knows that this is not really a studio, but a living room, even though a clay box stands in the corner, and next to it is a sculpture maquette covered with plastic film. What is called a villa is a seashore studio; outside the city, it is true, but not too far. Here live Aunt Olga, a new dog called Kinski and, between quarrels, Mother, too. Aunt Olga no longer has any money, for she

46

gave it all towards the building of a studio for Lion. Lion defends her against his mother and is now, with the support of his father, without asking his mother's help, arranging *emigration* for Aunt Olga too.

Suddenly she hears, through the roar of the television, Lion talking to someone in the kitchen. Her back jerks; she does not know whether she should hide somewhere (but where?) or stay here and see what happens.

She senses that the circle of light from the ceiling lamp is now falling on the kitchen table and also senses that mother and son are sitting in the darkness around it. The forgotten bread-knife reflects its own sparkle on to the words that are spoken at the table.

She swiftly finds herself a hiding place – climbs on to the window sill behind the curtain beside a plump aloe. The television ceremoniously raises its voice. The light of a street-lamp falls on to a red vase; its colour recalls a cold November sunset. In a drawer are letters from dead people, from many places on earth and in many languages. In another drawer are tin boxes full of forgotten and melancholy fruit sweets that have melted into brightly coloured lumps, a collection by a forbidden post-revolutionary Russian poet and, wrapped in lively tissue paper, a small ermine collar. The floor clicks.

Why does she not put on her sandals and creep quietly on her way? The only sound would be the slam as the front door shut. Whose heart it would echo in, and for how long, would no longer move her. Tomorrow, she would already be back in Tallinn as if she had come back from the moon. What does she care about Brezhnev's politics or human hearts, the meaning of the word OVIR or rumours concerning the persecution of the Jews. All of it would be to her as incomprehensible as the language of the birds and the animals.

A human shadow appears at the door, Lion himself. At once, he switches off the television, and although at first he does not see anything in the room, he does not switch on the light, but sits down on the floor in front of the covered clay statue and calls, whispering: 'Where are you? Come here!'

When she steps forward from the darkness, the figure sitting on the ground takes her hand without a word and presses it to the top of his head as if it were an eternal seal and not an earthly and treacherous human hand.

Brisk steps are heard from the corridor; the ceiling light flares on. In a moment she is standing face to face with the woman whose plait of hair she has slid through her hands without the remotest guess whose it is. For this reason she does not drop her gaze. It looks as if all the furniture is casting Lion curious glances from under its brows and waiting to see what he says. And not just the furniture.

Lion slowly rises to his feet, unwinds the film from the clay statue as if he were undressing a mummy and says, with such ceremony that the words could also be mocking: 'Mother, this is everything I told you about.' His mother steps a little farther away, as if she were taking part in some ancient game that she knows by rote, slits her eyes and remarks drily: 'Quite good, even in clay, very good. But don't you think it's a little too composed? To me that, look, that isn't very good, or that. You need to think about this. At the moment it is too, how to put it, too *unguarded*.' At the same time she steps from the form shaped in clay to the living shape in flesh and looks at it with interest from every side. But Lion says, relieved and weary, as if this, too, were part of the game: 'Stop it, mother. Enough already.'

The room grows quiet. Not even breathing can be heard. The top of mother's head reaches exactly to the level of her son's shoulder; her hair is still thick, but short, curly and grey. Her eyes are multi-coloured, although green has conquered brown. Their expression could perfectly well be called 'wild' if they were not so inquisitive and vigilant. Looking at these young, expressive, restless eyes, the question arises: where are the lace collar, the knee-socks and the white cuffs of the girl's school, and what ulterior motive lies behind the grey, Latvian blouse and the rich American sister-in-law's old skirt? Her handbag mother presses forcefully under her arm and coloured rays fly from her ring. It is certainly not made of glass.

Her son pushes his mother forward in front of the bared clay statue and its living model and says, not knowing to which: 'Remember, this is my mother.' But he warns his mother: 'Remember, this is your child.'

The boy's eyebrows are still wrinkled in warning, and his arms crossed on his chest in a challenge, when all at once his mother smiles her most dazzling smile. Although their own agreements and their own rules of play appear to apply between mother and son, at the same time it is clear that if the mother were some time to win, it would happen only by permission of the son.

At this moment the mother has a good opportunity. She throws her grey head upright and urges, as self-evidently as if all shirt-backs should be faded, all feet bare and all hair tousled: 'Du armes Kind, lass du dich umarmen.' Under Lion's vigilant gaze, there follows a moment of the warm scent of soap and lemon, as if the linen cupboard had reached out its hand and touched cheek to cheek. Then the moment is past and can no longer be retrieved.

No one knows what the time might be. All the glass beads of the chandeliers in the entire apartment are still tinkling, the folds in the curtains move compulsively as if someone were trying to make their exit between them. Somewhere, a tap is dripping.

Mother throws one more sofa cushion on top of the telephone and says: 'The next one goes at eleven fifteen. Lion, would you mind seeing me off,' and for a moment the childish loneliness of the old quavers in her voice. But Lion grasps the hand which, a moment ago, he pressed to the top of his head and announces: 'My call-up papers are in Mother's handbag.' Mother corrects him mechanically, with familiar irony: 'Your *cough-medicine* prescription, my darling.' Her son repeats, with the same irony, 'Yes, my *cough-medicine* prescription,' but he cannot conceal his questioning tone, and asks, hopefully and childishly, 'Mother, can you think of anything?' Mother repeats demandingly, as though she has not even heard the question: 'So you'll see me off, Lev?' But she does not leave her criticism unvoiced: 'Why do you ask, since you know very well that you have to give this prescription *under the counter*. You must give it to *Leo*, if *Leo* has not retired.'

In the hallway, the son takes his mother's shopping bag, secretly throws an anxious glance into the darkness of the room and encounters a smile which, taking into account the seriousness of the moment, is perhaps a little too broad.

Mother and son's footsteps still echo below on the paving as the silence of the apartment grasps her by the waist. When she switches off the lamp, the room is lit by the moon, as in ancient times. She pushes her hand out through the open window and writes with her finger on the pale air, as if in a school poetry book:

> The moon shines brightly,
> the dead drive lightly.
> My darling, have no fear!

Then she considers for a moment what to write next, and adds:

> In memoriam.
> 21 August 1968.

4

DO NOT stand at the window! DO NOT open the door! DO NOT answer the telephone! DO NOT move the furniture and DO NOT drag chairs across the floor. In the evening, DO NOT turn on the ceiling lamps, and when table lamps are switched on, DO NOT leave the curtains undrawn.

All her life she has wanted to hear these orders and prohibitions with her own ears. Their dangerous content has always seemed to her oh so enticing, frightening and sweet. She has always expected that for a change something might happen, a war might begin, a storm might come and blow the roofs off the houses, or at least that someone might die. She is tired of the fact that trains arrive on time, the fact that work begins and ends on time, that people hide their real desires.

In her pride, she believes she even knows the exact meaning of the words *informant, roundup* and NKVD, for as a child of the Fifties she has often, while hiding under the dinner table, listened to other people's secrets. At that time she also succeeded in seeing a real gun, and a big brown wardrobe that apparently saved someone's life, for during the bloodshed of 1941 a real Estonian father had lived there with his small son. The son caught diphtheria in the wardrobe and suffocated in his father's arms, but the father nevertheless somehow made his way to Sweden and, if he is not dead, lives there to this day.

But it seems to her that it was with that heavy, dark brown wardrobe in mind that Goethe wrote the ballad that is in all the readers about the desperate father and his sick son. In any case, she links information about secret hiding places and the NKVD's manhunts unerringly with the misty and obscure moors of the ballads across which the German father, pressing his sick son to his chest, eternally rides, and will continue to ride as long as the ballad remains on the school curriculum.

In summary, it can be remarked that the images she has of the years of oppression and human suffering are in general culled from books, which have nothing to do with real life. She knows, of course, exactly how everything ought to happen! Every single world war is preceded by a brilliant summer filled with tennis balls, dance music, the scent of eau de cologne and *café à la crème*, the rustle of trees and the glimmer of sea-water. No one in the whole world can yet imagine how fateful a number is 1914 or 1941; but wait, on the flowering bush there falls the shadow of a passing Alexander Blok or a newspaper-reading Thomas Mann; the seed of doubt is sown and soon the blossoms turn brown; the spa guests hurriedly travel home; phantoms appear in the sky like airships; signs and manifestations appear as Russian, German and American aeroplanes. Even the year 1968 is ready, biding its time.

The decades have flown past on the wings of a bird, and see! the August rain of 1968 is already pattering on the window panes. Over the city of Riga there hovers a dark cloud with glowing edges which recalls a drifting hymn book. Heavy rain scourges the waters of the river Daugava. A great fish rises to the surface for a moment, snaps up air-bubbles and mosquitoes and flies scourged limp by the rain, slaps the water with its tail and disappears down into its kingdom.

Lion opens his umbrella as soon as he steps out of the main door, but nevertheless the hem of his thin, pale coat is soaked immediately and darkens like the sand of a graveyard. He rushes through the pouring rain to the tram stop, turns on his heel, runs back, rushes up the stairs, searches too long for his key, gets the door open, leaves wet footprints everywhere like a dog, grabs his beloved penknife, which he had left behind in the house and which he always otherwise keeps with him and a notebook in which are recorded the addresses of two bronze-founders, the measurements and locations of a couple of available pieces of granite, the prices of pieces of marble and blocks of mahogany and, most important, the telephone number of a crane-operator. Tucked into the back cover of the notebook, by the way, is a mysterious dried lily-of-the-valley, a sweet and bitter reminder of the past summer and the initial G. This notebook is not for strangers' eyes. Lion leaves his things uttering the worn and ancient command: 'Keep them in order until my return! Wait!'

Yes, and now Lion must really hurry if he still wants to catch the Moscow train. He will be in time, if only he tries. If he breathes deeply. Through the nose, not the mouth! Not puffing like an animal, but quiet as a ghost! If his lungs do not draw, they must be pulled out! If his legs do not walk, they must be cut off!

As soon as the front door has shut after Lion, she goes to the window, knife and notebook still in her hands, and looks after Lion, not paying the slightest attention to the warning, 'It is forbidden to stand at the window!' How should she know that the great autumn hunt has already started and that sooner or later uniformed men may appear outside, men who shadow the hiding places and escape routes of people who are trying to dodge the draft. It would be no wonder if the hoarse rattle of the doorbell were to thwart the peace of the night with Field Green and Military Red! If she is unable to explain Lion's disappearance in any way to the uniformed man, then she must keep stumm and not unnecessarily give the impression that there is anyone in the apartment.

Thus she has now been buried alive on the fourth floor of a stone building from the Ulmanis period,* apartment number twenty-four, whose kitchen window has a distant view of a dark and enormous tree. The touch of yellow is not yet discernible in it at all. It is shiny from the rain and holds its own like a tin wreath or a gravestone. Thunderclouds and sleet clouds, dates and years disappear behind it as if they had never been. In the midst of the smoke, soot and lead of the sky, that tree is one and only, like the Lord, Your God. Through the window she sends the tree a long glance like an open postcard on which only a greeting is written. In the secret language, of course, it can mean something much more important and serious.

53

After that she makes a witch's circle through almost the whole apartment and chooses, individually and with enjoyment, the objects that she intends, now she is alone and will not disturb anyone, to examine more closely, for example three coloured volumes whose red bindings bear the label 'Alphonse Mucha', a blue volume, 'The Jewish Almanac', and a baize-green volume, 'Feodor Dostoyevsky'. These she pulls off the shelves and spreads out on the sofa, where, frivolously and brightly, they merge with the coloured cushions. Especially when seen from a distance.

But she cannot settle down, even yet, and must make another circuit of the apartment. This time she is halted by a calendar on the kitchen wall. To her great surprise, she has been away from Tallinn for scarcely two and a half days. What the calendar does not, of course, reveal is which is longer, a human day or a historic day.

If she did not know the date, she would now, as she looks out of the window, be ready to see November or even December – bushes that have dropped their leaves; snowdrifts, sheet ice and fur caps, and she is truly disappointed to see that the end of August is still in progress and that people are walking about quite happily with bare heads as if nothing has changed. She simply cannot believe that during her absence from Tallinn only two issues of the *Evening News* have appeared and that during this period only five trains have left Riga for Tallinn. It feels to her that over these two and a half days the summer has grown old and cold, like the eyes of those whose entire lives so far and the present decade have been compressed into just two days, yesterday and the day before. Here she exaggerates, as always, but that does not change things.

She stands there, helpless, before the calendar, and suddenly she thinks of the new raincoat which at this moment is hanging on a hook in Tallinn, very neglected and very empty, rustling to itself. It feels to her as if the coat is now living its own private life in Tallinn, doing precisely what it wants.

Lost in thought, she rummages in the pockets of her raincoat and feels between her fingers Lion's short, formal letter, written on the Artists' Union's official headed paper, in which Lion remembers himself to her uninterestingly (not omitting to mention in a couple of words an art exhibition held in Tallinn and the fact that they sat at the same table) and asks her 'if possible to sit as a model for four or five hours around 20 August in Riga'. The text seems to her now, naturally, absolutely ridiculous; it is directly linked with the bronze milkmaid and the head of Lenin, and she wonders how on earth it came about that she answered it.

Mentally ransacking the pockets of her own distant coat, she is not, by the way, searching for that crumpled letter, but for something completely different. In the pocket there must be, and is, a flat, white stone, washed by the sea. On the smoother side of the stone is scrawled a telephone number whose background still entrances her to the extent that she cannot restrain herself from, in her imagination, swapping Lion's eyes for another, considerably lighter pair. For some time she concentrates on their expression and shape and then does to those water-grey eyes something that thrifty and careful people do not do even with their buttons – she throws them away and at the same time forgets forever a telephone number, a genuinely Estonian first name and a white stone, which were so important two and a half days ago.

Far away in her thoughts, she has nevertheless constantly been eyeing an old, cobalt-blue soup tureen. It stands in the kitchen on the window sill and is filled with earth from which grows a blood-red cyclamen. The thick, multicoloured leaves, the half-open buds and the stiff, rigid flowers create an image of a fresh grave-mound standing on the window sill. The sky, the clouds and the roofs can be seen only over that grave-mound, heaped up with earth and generously decorated with flowers. The plant looks vigilant and dangerous, as if the spirit of the apartment, the guardian of the building or the hearth-spirit were hidden in its roots. It is worth looking after that plant, and that is indeed what she does. Strokes its flowers and leaves with her cheek, like a cat. Then she goes and sits, satisfied, on the sofa, opens all three books she has taken from the shelf; she does not leaf through any of them however, but *begins to wait.*

She has no idea whether the Leo who has the power to order Lion's *personal records* to be moved from *one compartment* to another is, in terms of military rank and position, one of the main angels of the heavenly forces, or an ordinary soldier. Neither has she the faintest clue or image of the methods or vocabulary of the conscription officials. There is only one magical phrase she understands, and that is: 'Unfit for permanent service in time of peace.'

Leo's place of residence is in the Capital itself, beyond many mountains and many rivers, on the other side of barracks and workers' quarters, on the other side of boiler rooms, glass collection points, gas pipes and blood donation stations. What Leo in Moscow wishes is done in Riga. Just a telephone call. Leo certainly knows how things are fixed.

The only condition of success is that Lion should himself make an appearance before Leo. He must not look furtively from beneath his eyebrows, like some Finn, or smile silently and too much, like a Chinese. He absolutely must convey Aunt Olga's greetings, and at the same time, with the greetings, hold out an old but very clear photograph showing the six-year-old Leo hand-in-hand with the four-year-old Aunt Olga. Aunt Olga, too, has cute dimples in her cheeks, of course, but what about this little Leo, he is nothing but butter and comb honey. In a word – Lion's fate now hangs on two former child-faces and memories, if these exist. If they are now at all to find their way through the double door into Leo's room beneath the picture of Brezhnev.

An angel accompanies Lion for part of his journey toward Leo. Suddenly he appears straight out of the air on to the higher, empty bunk of the sleeping compartment, and the brilliance of his glory sets the weak tea in the cheap tea-glass of the Baltic rail administration sparkling in a quite extraordinary and meaningful way. Swaying, the train crosses the Valdai plain; the glasses clink rhythmically in their tin holders, flakes of soot fall on to the greyish pillowcase. Lion pulls back the sheets and turns his face to the wall. He tries to anticipate the following day, but however hard he tries he sees only one image. It is made of the cheapest and most terrifying material the world has to offer – flesh and bone.

The train sways. The passengers are already asleep. Above the secrets of sleep there hangs a thick coverlet which, since the death of Doctor Freud, no one has dared raise. How many hectares of mud and truck wheel-marks, how many cubic metres of factory waste, how many cubic metres of logs left to rot are already between this train and Riga station. The infinite plains sigh with uncut hay, lorries clatter along muddy roads carrying frozen pig carcasses who knows where. Even the potatoes in the fields are so stunted that it is as if divine blessing has been withheld from them.

But all these plains and distances can, after all, be nothing but imagination and conjuring tricks, the delirium of a business traveller. The capitals of the Baltic countries remain in their places even if any number of trains disappear into the distances. In position, too, stands the clay box in the living room of the Riga apartment. It is worth looking more closely at that clay, for it is more alive than any clay that has hitherto been seen. It has been warmed day after day by Lion's own hands, crushed so long that it has changed from a cold, dead lump into a substance which can be made into a body and, if all goes well, a soul and even a shadow.

It is, then, no wonder that, as she thinks about Lion, she goes to the clay box and presses the mark of her hand into the clay. The mark looks as helpless and frightening as a cave painting. She looks at it, dissatisfied and critical, and then presses the mark of her mouth next to it. To do this, she must kneel. Perhaps this is a seal and a promise. It is, at least, a kiss. Perhaps a kiss whose taste is frankly political.

She is familiar with only two political terms – they are *war* and *peace*. With all her heart, she despises the freshers' political debates and young people's discussion circles in which short-haired boys got up like working-class youths and strong country-maid-type girls try strenuously to make sense of the future of the world. But she is defiantly, without any sensible arguments, of the opinion that the future of her world is different.

57

A certain Russian boy who is considered an *underground genius* once showed her, across the table in a café, a copy of *Doctor Zhivago*, wrapped in newspaper. Rumours of *secret circulars* and *plain-clothes men* she considers exaggeration and bluff, although she has heard that Joseph Brodsky (who lives in Leningrad) and Paul-Eerik Rummo* (of whom no one knows exactly where he lives) can be *called in for interrogation* for the dissemination of particular poems. Those words – *called in for interrogation* – she repeats, carefree and mechanical as a parrot, and other people like her nod their heads, equally carefree and mechanical. Being called in for interrogation sounds almost as vague and grand as the Finnish Winter War, the Hungarian Uprising, the Three Baltic States.

Some people, however, know enough to say that you would not *get your teeth knocked out* for the sake of Brodsky or Paul-Eerik, but for what reason this might occur no one knows. If only they did! Perhaps you might *get your teeth knocked out* when you have innocently given your mouth to Lev, whose secret first name is Lion? Her complete lack of expertise she has, just like the others, concealed behind a particular ambiguous smile and random phrases that have lodged in her mind. Boldly she has spoken words as to whose real meaning she hasn't a clue.

The whips the Angel of the Lord prepared long ago now whistle through the air. The Angel is already experimenting. But she frivolously thinks the whistling comes from the radio, whose howling has already for some time been audible from downstairs through the ventilation window. Something is in the air.

She becomes restless and, without any particular intention, puts her sandals on. Her wide belt could equally well be from officer Mars's wardrobe as from pickpocket Mercury's; this she pulls one hole tighter around her waist, and is quite pleased with what she sees in the mirror.

All at once it becomes clear that it was indeed the right time to twirl in front of the mirror fully dressed, as the front door, closed with a well-oiled lock, opens quietly, as if by itself, the draught makes the glass beads of the chandelier tinkle again, and in steps

Father. He appears like lightning from out of a blue sky. The cuffs of Father's shirt are as white as his teeth. Father is probably not as easy to drive off the rails as many perhaps think. The hand Father holds out in greeting must be accepted, for he holds out his hand only seldom. And if he does so, it is not certain whether he does it out of courtesy or whether it is his peculiar form of mockery. Probably only that slightly simple officer Mars can clip Father's wings, while the other gods, foremost among them the shifty Mercury, simply blow more wind under them.

Lion has not told her that his Father has arrived in Riga from the other side of the Iron Curtain, where his permanent residence is located. Perhaps it is better not to know absolutely everything! Nevertheless, she is amazed. If only the peaceful canton of Thurgau, filled with flowers and cows, had been mentioned earlier with even half a word – Thurgau, from where it is only a couple of hours' journey to Milan, Paris and Munich, but to where a postcard from Riga takes three or perhaps even six months.

How could she know that the phrase dropped by Mother, 'Father came from Kaunas and brought some fresh country butter,' actually meant that Father arrived from Munich, bringing with him fresh news *from the West*. (Which, it is true, was outdated at once when the quite *bloody Eastern* news arrived in the morning.)

Because of Kaunas and the country butter, she has formed her very own idea of Father, which does not fit reality in the least. Father *does not have* a chequered market bag in his hand, a hump on his shoulder or gold teeth in his mouth. Father does speak Russian perfectly, it is true, but in a foreign way, rolling his 'r's. The fresh scent of Chanel pour Monsieur which rises from Father is in itself a considerable blow to the image of a market bag and gold teeth. But an even greater blow is the glint in Father's eye, which throws a sparkling light from his face to his delicate-skinned hands. Those eyes notice everything, bind together all loose ends, laugh and tease, and are quite inaccessible even though they are enticing. They are like those lively brown birds

59

that fly innocently from one bush to the next, but which, if one follows them, can easily lead to a strange land where humans do not lightly set foot.

Things are going well for Father. Every day, things just go better for Father. Father breathes peacefully, always counts to ten first, controls situations. On the border of the Evil Empire, he always looks taciturn uniformed guards straight in the eye, and he always gets through customs without baggage-searches. His own family, however, Father has not managed to get out of the Empire, although no one is directly against it and he is still given polite promises. This time Kuzminitchna will receive a soft pink woollen sweater, a handbag for her daughter and a new Japanese miracle drug for her diabetic old mother.

It becomes clear that his son's difficult, old-fashioned and literary name was given him at his Father's command. The son is, in any case, his Father's darling and the apple of his eye, his weak spot. Or, to put it more eloquently – the son is his Father's daughter, and for him his Father would hunt down a firebird, for example, or bring back for him under his coat from beyond the seas a fire-red flower with its roots. Until now, the son has not needed a firebird or a fire-red flower, chewing gum or ball-point pens. Now, then, quite suddenly, at an impossible moment, when there are other things to worry about, the son, a Jew, needs this Estonian!

The boy Lion has spoken privately with Father. Without the knowledge of his mother, but advised and supported by Aunt Olga, he has given Father an order to go to the city apartment and to talk to the creature who has appeared there from who-knows-where as *honestly* and *directly* as to his own child. He is not to frighten her, he is to choose the simplest words, to speak slowly and calmly. To repeat questions, if need be. He is to behave unaffectedly and amicably, as with Kaspar Hauser. He is to talk primarily about *practical matters*, as no one but Father knows how to talk about them so clearly. About OVIR too, of course. And he is not to appear before his son without a certain clear and direct, conventional and romantic word: *yes*. The boy's request is as merciless as the human heart.

Father's predicament is, however, greater than he is allowing to show at this moment. Father does not know where to start. And he is not even sure which language is understood here. He tries nevertheless, pulling out from under the table a hard, uncomfortable chair with an animal's paws as feet; he offers the chair and sits down on the other side of the table. He uses the formal mode of address. Digs up from deep in his memory the key-word 'Estonia' and tries to link it with some image or at least names and figures, but nothing comes to mind apart from a faded page of photographs from the Efron-Brockhaus encyclopaedia showing men with furs round their necks and ears and women in cardigans standing, basket in hand, sturdy legs set wide apart under their striped skirts, with eyes as blue as summer flowers. Father has a feeling that the Efron encyclopaedia may have remarked as follows about the Estonians: 'Peasants (and paid estate workers, practitioners of many forms of artisanship) in the governments of Estonia and Livonia. A higher spiritual life is absent.' On the basis of this information, Father covertly concludes that Estonians still light their way with torches and dress in lambskin. This being the case, it is understandable that, as he looks around the room, Father feels great relief on account of the fact that nowhere does he see birch-baskets, fur caps, cardigans, torches or sheep.

As if in answer to his own remote-from-life imaginings, Father says something completely different from what he had intended. He says: 'All of this is nothing; there are much more important matters.' These words, surprising to both interlocutors, are strengthened by the sparkling of the fan of light in the bottom of the mirror and the overlong silence.

Then, however, Father leans unwillingly against the back of the chair. His face remains in shadow, as if in some indifferent scene in a play depicting an event by the name of 'interrogation'. Father now begins to ask questions which are so formal that even he wonders at their content as he makes them audible. 'Are your friends and relatives (the cautious and general words *friends* and *relatives*, not the presumptuous and concrete *friend* and *parents*) not concerned about your departure from home?' How can Father restrain himself from adding: 'And you are so young!' This remark is, however, obviously quite excessive, for as she hears it the defendant swings her legs, hurt, although she now tries an expression which she has learned to use very fluently, both in Estonian and in Russian. She announces: 'I am extremely independent!' If it has worked on a dried fish like the main ideologist of a Soviet republic, after all, why shouldn't it work on one miserable Father?

She is unable to celebrate her triumph over Father for very long, however, for Father immediately draws his chair back toward the table, pulls himself together, forms phrases which are really clear and short, speaks in a clear, friendly and encouraging voice until he finally reaches his goal – to determine in his own heart what kind of a creature he is dealing with, and what that creature really wants of the future. The more friendly and clear the questions Father asks, the more indeterminate the shrugs of the shoulders he receives in answer. But the shrugs do not fit in the least with the vigilant and self-confident gaze that accompanies them.

Gradually Father leaves the clear and short sentences aside and also forcibly prizes away the image of torches and sheep. In the style of a pathos-laden soap-box orator, he asks: 'Do you really believe that in that language which is, how shall I put it, without perspectives, yes,' he purringly emphasises, 'without perspective,' and then continues fluently: 'it is possible to express all new ideas and all old and new feelings?'

Father likes the answer; it rings out as moving and protestant as if it came from the mouth of a member of confirmation school: 'I do!' But this is not the answer Father expects. So Father presses both his light pianist's hands to his eyes and sits quietly for some time, lost in thought. All that is audible is his breathing, which confirms that Father is alive and carries the burden of his life with difficulty, like everyone else.

When Father finally raises his head, neither his cool scent of eau de cologne, his inaccessible smile nor his recent questions mean anything any longer. Before the future, they are temporary, and pass by like a day or a moment. The performance is over. When Father now orders: 'Look me in the eye!', she cannot but look, and merely shrugs her shoulders. In the corner crouches the Angel of Darkness, leafing through a notebook in a neutral-looking way. The clock ticks more loudly, water drips from the bathroom tap more noisily, quicksilver gleams under the glass. The gazes of both are equally merciless.

Father is the one who rises from the other side of the table and leans both hands on the table so solidly that the table shudders as if a spirit has been damned. Father says curtly, threateningly and without any comprehensible link with what has gone before: 'Well, then. Let it be as you wish.' And adds, in a dry and official tone: 'Remember that I had to say exactly the same words to my son Lion at two o'clock last night.'

The blue woods and white clover of Estonia suddenly stream away to an infinite and unfathomable distance. The blind abyss of a strange life murmurs close by, straight ahead, and every moment it threatens to break over her head. Blood rises to her cheeks without her knowing why, and she covers her cheeks with her hair as if Father had caught her in the act. It may indeed be that Father knows something about children enticed to forest clearings and of the tempter's triumph, which is so sweet that it leaves everything else in shadow.

Without allowing to show what he senses or does not sense, knows or does not know, Father continues his peculiar, one-sided conversation, little as it has to do with sensible talk about practical matters. Father leaves a certain allegory untold, a story which he also told his son Lion during the night. Father advises: 'You can remind each other of this story in the future,' and adds drily, 'Assuming, of course, that there is a future.'

As he speaks, Father compares the time shown by his watch with that shown by the wall-clock. Father's story is short, and not particularly new.

In a particular village an old, poor couple live on charity with their son. They are the most wretched old people that have ever been seen. Their son is a rough-natured man, does heavy work and earns little money, as the custom generally is. In addition to his old parents, he also has a wife and five children to feed. One day, when the old people have decided to go into the forest to die, the door opens and into the cabin steps a strange man with a white monkey. The man wants to get rid of the monkey. The old people do not want the monkey; they have nothing to give the monkey to eat, as there is nothing in the house but an empty flour-sack. The man explains in honeyed words that this is no rare monkey, but the very same white monkey of which everyone has heard at least something at some time in their lives. This is the monkey that can fulfil all wishes, whatever they are. And there are always wishes; why shouldn't there be? The old people, who just a moment ago were against accepting the monkey, now begin to negotiate in whispers, and the stranger waits humbly, cap in hand. The monkey's eyes shine and its tail swishes like a cat's. Then their negotiations are over. The old people say, shyly, that they want two hundred francs in cash. With that sum, they can survive until their deaths without having to eat bread earned by their son. They have hardly said the words when there is a knock at the door and in steps an official bringing two hundred francs in life insurance and news of their son's death.

Father leaves unsaid: 'If you wish for something, beware of the fulfilment of your wish;' such naked moralising he considers tasteless. But he makes a pause suitable to this moment and gazes at the long, bleached, sharp eyelashes, behind which there flashes a small flame that provokes wonderment. Slender fingers have already for some time been playing with a pencil whose lead is broken. Eyeing the fingers and the flame, Father finds it necessary to provide comfort, clumsily and unaccustomedly: 'There, there!' The consolation sounds like a warning.

Immediately afterwards, Father throws a compulsive gaze toward the telephone, which is still covered with a cushion, and asks too clearly, in too loud a voice: 'What was I really looking for in this room? Why did I come?' Both question and answer are very clearly intended for the walls, which have ears. The answer is: 'Well, of course. I was supposed to take two bottles of Armenian cognac from the crockery cupboard.' After this, Father makes the cupboard door creak just like in a radio play and lifts out of the darkness two bottles of cognac, holds them by the neck for a moment like dead chickens and then wraps them in brown paper.

After this, there is another comparatively long pause. She expects Father to leave now, but Father does not leave; it is as if he were waiting for someone who should arrive at any moment. She does not really know how to relate to Father – sometimes he seems to her too young, then again too old, sometimes difficult and frightening but at the same time ordinary and broken by sorrow. Wavering he is, in any case.

It cannot be denied that she doubts whether this man is a father at all. Who else then, she does not know. If she were not *politically* so *illiterate*, she could even think Father was a *KGB* man. But of the KGB she knows as little as of life beyond the grave. Sometimes she wonders how Father got into the apartment. From abroad! Even though she heard with her own ears how Father's key opened the lock of the front door, she does not consider it entirely impossible that Father appeared from behind the curtains or from the third room. She has only cast the occasional glance into the third room, and only as she passed by its door, which is ajar. Who knows what room it really is. At the same time she remembers the warning that *plain-clothes men* should not be allowed in. What if Father is a *plain-clothes man*? There is no one to ask.

Finally she even begins to wonder whether the children playing hopscotch and shrieking in shrill voices down in the yard are just any old children, or whether they are merely acting out the roles of hopscotch-playing children, thereby fulfilling some secret state role of which perhaps only the child-carer knows something, if she really is a child-carer. And those two old ladies down on the bench beside the door look too genuine, as if they were sitting there on the bench with some ulterior motive in mind. The real life of the state may be, to the glance of an accidental witness, as secret as life beyond the grave.

She sits there on a strange chair at a strange table, her chin in her hand, rolls the pencil absent-mindedly on the table and believes she is the only one in the world who knows what the human heart is.

Night and day divide the world into East and West like a black wall and a white wall, like forgetting and laughter, from which all calls for help rebound. Between the curtains a strip of blue Livonian sky can be seen; in the sky stands a small white cloud, as unreal and remote from life as a book-cover or a page in an art-book. Would that distant old cloud care anything for the bones of the dead in the earth, the bones of the living in flesh, whirlwinds in the street, the newspaper on the table or the biography of General Yershov, who commands all Brezhnev's forces in Prague.

In the yard there slouches a man with a white monkey – he is either coming or going.

5

It must be remembered that opening the front door of this apartment is always followed by the cold tinkle of glass beads. You have to get used to it. There is no point in trembling when the door opens.

Although Father is expecting Aunt Olga, he jumps when the curtain moves and a sharp tinkle of glass is heard through the room. On stepping in, Aunt Olga fills the entire apartment with life and movement. First of all, without looking at the room and without a thought for who is there, she directs her steps to the kitchen. For in the twinkling of an eye the thudding of opening and shutting cupboard doors, the clatter of crockery and the running of water begin to be heard, prosaic and familiar sounds of everyday life which are able to extinguish doubts and question marks from the air.

Claws scraping, Kinski the dog rushes into the living room. He is as smooth, shiny and spotted as a pike or perch; he wags his tail, which has been cut precisely as short as its family tree and the regulations concerning tail-cutting allow, at Father as a mark of acquaintance. Beneath his black dog-lips, teeth in exemplary condition are revealed. A heavy ruff falls on to his white chest. On his broad boxer's face is the melancholy and impressive gaze of a managing director. Only briefcase and spectacles are missing. Since fate has not provided Kinski the dog with hands, he now raises his paw and scratches energetically at Father's knee until he finally understands that he is required to undo the buckle of his collar. At that moment Kinski loses all interest in Father, disappears, sighing heavily, beneath the table, rests his chin gloomily on his paws and stays there, gazing with deep prejudice at a strange pair of sandals within which bare toes move.

It is only now that Aunt Olga makes time to come into the room, her hands wet and a drying-up cloth on her shoulder. Aunt Olga turns out to be surprisingly voluminous and thick-set and resembles, in both appearance and expression, a large flower of the common man, a dahlia or ox-eye daisy. Her hair, which is cut short at her ears, is combed straight over her head; it is as clean and white as the wimple of a sister of mercy. At the top of her head, it is kept in order by a convex brown hair-comb. Such combs were worn by old people in the Fifties; they were made in Russian and Ukrainian factories, and were unusually cheap in price. Thus it is a miracle that Aunt Olga does not also wear brown striped schoolgirls' stockings.

As Aunt Olga glances at Father, her eyes say clearly that Father is her younger, cherished and beloved brother, in whose every movement and word Aunt Olga finds ever new and fresh causes for delight. In general it looks as if it is not very difficult to delight Aunt Olga. She is delighted by clear weather, a polite shop assistant in the dairy, a new bud on a house-plant, Lion's appetite and Mother's new shoes. Everyone has seen Aunt Olga. Aunt Olga always knows what to do if a child or dog gets lost in the crowd, if someone has a nose-bleed or something in their eye, if a black car drives up to the front door at night, if socks and underwear are unavailable and if sugar, too, is rationed, or if there is a death in the house.

Aunt Olga steps into the room as easily as if she had left it only five minutes ago. Now she seems to be interested only in the potted aloe on the window sill. She carefully touches the earth with her finger-tip, takes a long-spouted watering can from behind the curtain and pours water carefully and tenderly into the pot. Her movements are slow and certain, like someone who knows exactly what has been, what is and what will be.

As she passes the girl sitting at the table, Aunt Olga pats her on the shoulder encouragingly, as if she were one of her own. Her brother, or Father, however, she grasps by the hand, and although Father, through old, life-long resistance, resists, Aunt Olga has her way, as always. Father goes with her into the kitchen. What is said there, she never knows. But it may be very important, since Kinski the dog also emerges quickly from under the table, yawns, stretches, and then disappears, smacking his lips, in the direction of the kitchen, ignoring the girl who remains in the room.

First of all, having been left alone, she yawns comfortably like the dog, and stretches her limbs. Immediately afterwards she listens for what is happening in the kitchen. Nothing is to be heard. Not even the rumble of speech. It feels as if everything that is to be done has now been done. It is possible that all negotiations have been negotiated, all discussions finished and all agreements signed. Perhaps even in blood. Anything is possible.

The corners of the room seem ash-grey and absolutely unfamiliar. Outside, the next raincloud is already in place. At that moment Aunt Olga arrives in the room again and calls her as naturally as if she did so every day: 'Well, my girl, come and drink your tea!' But it has to be said that at the same time there is in Aunt Olga's voice a suspicion of irony, which may of course originate with Father.

The blood-red cyclamen on kitchen window sill throws its own glimmer into the lively motion of Father's hands. Aunt Olga does not pour tea from an ordinary and everyday teapot, but from a very special and rare porcelain one whose convex white sides are decorated with crossed swords and gold coats of arms. Glanced at superficially, it could easily be believed that the sides of the teapot are decorated with thigh-bones and skulls. On the table, the sugar gleams as white as the rough white sand of the Baltic. Spoons and teeth clink against the edges of cups.

Father and Aunt Olga exchange glances. Aunt Olga begins to speak, as they have earlier agreed. She says: 'Now Lion will no longer return to us.' She for whom the message is intended asks, in accordance with the script, feeling real and unaffected fear: 'Why?'

But Aunt Olga's reply comes from a quite different time and different place. That time and that place are buried beneath the ruins of yesterday's world. Long ago, concrete and asphalt have been poured over them, car parks have been laid out, offices and department stores built. But of course that is not Aunt Olga's fault. For that reason, Father does not even raise his eyebrows as Aunt Olga gives voice to her ceremonial answer, dug up from beneath the ruins: 'Because it is you who are now his home, not us.'

Under the weight of that old-fashioned response, it is not possible to do anything but lean your bare, sharp elbows on the tea-table. At the same time you must take the butter knife in your hand and draw with its point, in the smooth lump of butter sleeping in the white earthenware dish, eyes and a mouth, and a nose with a moustache under it. Aunt Olga follows her actions in amazement; she cannot remember seeing anything like it at any tea table. But Aunt Olga's confusion amuses Father, as always.

Then the lump of butter is smoothed even again, like *Brezhnev's History of the State* or a parking place. It is quite possible that everything that happened was simply Aunt Olga's imagination. In any case, Aunt Olga's eyes, as she runs them over the damaged slab of butter, are as innocently curious as if life, for them, were nothing but some film by Fellini or Visconti. Like prose with a certain number of pages. Like poetry, in which fees are calculated on a different basis. Like a question of style.

Father follows the conversation of those eyes silently. From his expression one may note that he knows a thing or two about it. Then Father thanks Aunt Olga for the tea, jokingly accepts Kinski the dog's paw – the dog has wearied each of those sitting at the table by offering it to them in turn – and fetches from the living room his briefcase, with the clinking cognac bottles. With Aunt Olga Father talks in simple phrases which, without a knowledge of the secret language, one cannot, even with the best will in the world, understand.

Over Aunt Olga's shoulder, Father's gaze slides farther than one might imagine; perhaps it slides as far as the courtyard, where a strange man is lurking with his white monkey. Father smiles helplessly, his face twitches strangely, he stops speaking in the middle of a word, and has disappeared before Aunt Olga has time to give him her bag, filled with heavy milk-bottles, to take to the villa.

70

The rain-cloud has continued its travels once again; the evening sun glimmers on the side of the tea-pot and lends a shine to distant roofs and window-panes. The rivers Daugava, Neeme and Vistula glow in this light like an absolutely new, shiny piece of barbed wire which binds entire countries and peoples to the Baltic Sea. The radio has promised cold weather from the Arctic Sea up in the north all the way down to the south.

Father's sudden departure has, after all, offended Aunt Olga. A treat will probably help. In Aunt Olga's life, such things can be arranged on a whim. To the great disappointment of Kinski the dog, a pot of home-made peach jam appears from the refrigerator, is ceremoniously divided between two shallow glass bowls, and chocolate chips are sprinkled on top.

Aunt Olga's preserve is, for her, as great a struggle as the ironed sheets and the big jar of cherry sauce. She feels as if she has fallen down from the moon; otherwise she would already know that she who fights most ardently against preserves is she to whom preserves taste best.

The delight of eating destroys the indefinite shadow, which slips on to the ceiling and the walls. It feels as if low black clouds were hurrying one after the other just beneath the window. Nevertheless the sky already looks completely clear, and although clouds are on their way, they are still below the horizon.

Suddenly, despite the interdiction, she puts her head out of the window, looks to the left and the right, using the opportunity to her advantage like a thief, and fills her lungs with fresh air. Directly across the road, an old, brown wooden house is burning. Black smoke and red flames rise from the roof. The smoke casts shadows on the kitchen walls. The building burns as prosaically as if its burning were completely ordinary and there were nothing to fear about it. Of course she knows quite accurately what a real conflagration looks like. This thing here does not look like anything much. It does not bring to mind lengthy depictions of burning houses. If it brings anything to mind, then it is drawings by mad people.

She is amazed that Aunt Olga takes the fire so seriously. Aunt

Olga stands by the window as if rooted to the spot, and the red of the fire and the black of the smoke are reflected in blotches on her white hair. Lord knows what Aunt Olga now sees and how much she has seen before. In any case, Aunt Olga has now completely forgotten the person who, disappointed with the fire, sits back down at the table and, following the shadows of the smoke, indulges herself by taking juice from the preserve straight from the jar. For it does not occur to her that that burning building could be someone's home and that Aunt Olga might even know them.

Smoke and fumes flow in through the open window. Perhaps at this very moment party clothes, pot plants, cushions, quilts and beds are burning. A pink babe-in-arms has been brought out of the house, and it wriggles on the asphalt in the midst of the random hubbub. From time to time the child lets out ringing cries of joy.

In the smoke from this fire there gradually materialises, soon is made visible at its natural size, a certain spring day in 1984. On that day she has just planted, with her own hands, ten large, multi-coloured sweet-pea seeds. She writes down all ten pedantically in her notebook, for all ten have already germinated, and by the time July comes they will have put forth a large number of tendrils and blossoms.

She casts a satisfied glance at the mysterious strip of earth, inhales the scents of the May day and goes upstairs to the attic. There she begins enthusiastically to rummage through the book-boxes that contain old schoolbooks, ancient children's books such as *Winnie the Pooh* and *Alice in Wonderland*, the *History Textbook of the Communist Party of the Soviet Union*, a picture book entitled *Egg* and *Anatomy for the VIIIth form*. As she opens it, she can see once again the old skeleton grinningly presenting its hip-bones and rib-cage, which can be seen through a bra that has been drawn on in red and a blue ring on its fourth finger.

On the face of the person looking at the picture of the skeleton there appears a strange, timeless expression, as if the intervening years have simply flown past her without hitting her, like bullets from a gun. Even if one of them really had hit her, for example the year 1968, she herself has cut it free of her flesh, put it in a tin box, and looks at it from time to time with the experienced eyes of a romantic. Compared to what is to come, it is not even worth speaking of 1968. But the Angel of the Lord looks straight through the arrogant words and does not say what he sees.

But she sees, through the newly painted gable window of the new attic, bare trees and black songbirds. From below in the yard heavy footsteps are heard, for the father and son who are walking around the house are looking happily at the results of their labour – a house totally clad in resinous white boards. This house is their own, flesh of their flesh and blood of their blood. But they are not this father and this son. They are not Jews but Estonians. Not in Riga but on the island of Vorms in the Baltic Sea. So much time has now marched forward that Chernenko has now been raised to the throne of Brezhnev's Kingdom. Two great funerals have been held; everyone still remembers the thump of the heavy coffin, which passed with the speed of the wind throughout the entire Kingdom. New plans are hatched. A campaign is in progress for the removal of summer cottages throughout the state. But on this island one summer-house is being built. The entire courtyard can be seen from its attic window, and everything that is said there can be heard.

She puts the book illustration of the skeleton to her ear and pricks her ears. A third man has arrived in the courtyard, a stranger, not accompanied by a white monkey but carrying armfuls of pea-stakes which he has cut from the bushes below. The townies disguised as countryfolk, the *summer visitors*, all examine the house's new cladding.

Suddenly the new arrival says, without any further introduction: 'Well, now there's a clear edict from Moscow. We'll see if they'll start taking our houses away or what.' Father replies: 'Well, damn it, let them try!' and strikes his new axe into the ground.

With the pale blue northern sky behind them, the three men stand gritting their teeth, their necks stiff. There they have stood since the times of the Order of the Brethren of the Sword, throughout the whole Great Northern War and the Great Famine,

73

in their teeth always one and the same threat: 'I will set fire to my house myself before giving it up!' That threat has nestled in tinder and flint, torches and tow, petrol-cans and cigarette ends. Now it is kept in breast pockets with a cigarette lighter and preserved as a can of petrol in the corner of the garage. You never know when it will be needed again.

If that threat has been learned along with your mother tongue, the ruins of a fireplace and empty foundations feel quite homely; or, to put it more accurately, they do not make any kind of impression. They are a self-evident part of the landscape of the homeland. Without the ruins of a hearth and empty foundations, the Estonian landscape would lose some of its own message, the secret thought of its existence. Where else could such frightening weeds and such cursed buttercups grow than in the kingdoms between the Baltic and the Danube that have disappeared from the map? Weeds and buttercups fracture road surfaces and steps, graves sink through the ground under their own weight, they even flourish in eaves and guttering and between roof-tiles. Roofs leak in the rain, cats and beggars piss on the steps, a church tower can be made out far into the Baltic over the multilingual dejection. A city like a delirious image or the island of the dead. But excessive lyricism is extinguished as soon as one looks more closely. Heavy lorries are already spattering overcoats with mud, cranes are creaking; life is on the boil. Even the Angel of the Lord smiles as impenetrably as the secretary of a local committee. There is no escape. Whatever happens to people, starlings have to come back here every summer, for there is nowhere else for them to go. Everywhere else has its own starlings.

There is a strong wind. White and black birds' wings trap the air-currents. Through the Estonian threats and curses, the joyful and mocking chirruping of the starlings is heard. 'I'll set fire to it with my own hands,' the men threaten. At the same time they cannot stop themselves from checking that the corners are true and the cladding is straight. One swears: 'Look, damn it, it's crooked under the window,' and another mutters, 'You're talking nonsense!' Then the men are quiet, strike the cladding, and, feeling hidden fear and mistaken and exaggerated arrogance, they gaze at the large white building like a naked woman or an empty coffin.

A little up from this building, to the north, are the foundations of a burned rectory which, in forty years, have grown full of spruces, moss and liverwort. The branches of lilac trees planted by the dead have wound themselves around spruce branches in a picturesque way. Behind the foundations is an untouched stony strand where twice a day, at set times, soldiers appear, accompanied by weapons and bloodhounds. There must be order. Tak poloyeno. Ordnung muss sein.

Above is Åland and its islands, down in the south is the city of Riga. Riga is as far away as Stockholm. Moscow is closer, that Moscow with which the men have living links, strengthened during sauna evenings with spirits and beers. What Moscow believes itself to be and what can be expected of it, that the men know. But Stockholm's time has not yet come. Or else it is long past. Damn it, do shirt-sleeves fray there too, and is car-metal as soft as it is here? Is it possible that the weather changes there too, that starlings whistle and people get backache?

Every time the men look north, toward Stockholm, they see two muddy caterpillar tractor treads, the foundations of a ruined barn; they see the trees of the island and the nest of a starling that returns to its eggs when the house is set alight.

Years are linked to one another like human vertebrae. She who hears the threat to burn in 1984 has seen the fire of 1968. There she is, still licking her bowl of preserves and gazing at Aunt Olga's broad back, which covers everything, the entire view from the window. It may be that everything that can be seen cannot, after all, be distinguished with the naked eye.

Finally, however, Aunt Olga turns her back to the view and sighs as heavily as if she had just seen from the window Berlin's Kristallnacht or the great Odessa pogrom. Fortunately, Aunt Olga is liberated from her sad thoughts by her own heavy shopping bag, from whose depths she lifts up a magnificent bunch of grapes, rinsing its long, yellow-green, glassy grapes under running water.

Then Aunt Olga sets the shining bunch of grapes on a platter as tenderly and gently as if she had grown them herself in her own vineyard, blown them out of molten glass or brought them with her from the land of Canaan.

Outside, on the other side of the road, the fire has meanwhile been put out, God be praised. Black ash continues to fly through the air. Aunt Olga now breaks grapes off the bunch and handles them contentedly. Aunt Olga has no questions. Unlike Father. But she has found a new listener, to whom she wants to tell Dostoyevsky's dream. It looks as if Dostoyevsky's dream is Aunt Olga's property, which moth does not eat nor rust destroy. For this reason Aunt Olga tells Dostoyevsky's dream very seldom, and on very particularly important days. This dream was one of Lion's great childhood fears.

The day has been, in Aunt Olga's opinion, so important that she could not possibly leave the dream untold. It is not known whether she tells it on account of the call-up order or because something is happening in East and West. This dream, or rather, more accurately, its telling, means the same to Aunt Olga as *ash and eggs, sorrow that is too deep to be expressed in words* have meant to the entire Jewish people.

It is most likely that Aunt Olga wants to recount Dostoyevsky's dream today simply because of the sunburnt, tousle-headed phantom that has unexpectedly appeared from who-knows-where, mixed up their way of life and is now rocking on a chair by the kitchen table and stroking the chest of Kinski the dog.

Aunt Olga approaches the dream quietly and wisely, as if it did not matter. First she relates what she saw on Tuesday when she went to the other side of the Lielupe river. What business Aunt Olga had on the other side of the Lielupe river and where the Lielupe river might be situated remains obscure, despite explanation. The gaps between Aunt Olga's words, if there are any, can be filled as you wish.

As already mentioned, Aunt Olga begins from far away, from valerian root, which she sometimes, familiarly, refers to as *valerianka*, sometimes, significantly and mysteriously, as the root of mortal terror. It becomes clear that every summer Aunt Olga makes two journeys to the other side of the Lielupe river. The first and more cheerful she makes, as the lime-trees bloom and the sun shines, to gather linden blossoms. The second, more sombre, she makes as the valerian roots are already drying and as night creeps, during brightest day, under the bushes. This is what she did on Tuesday. Aunt Olga set off on her journey early, carrying in her basket, as always, a plasterer's trowel and an old pair of leather gloves. The trowel is for digging the roots up and the gloves for gathering them and removing earth from them; they are, in other words, not intended for the practising of secret freemasonry rites, as one might easily conclude from following Aunt Olga's expressions.

Aunt Olga has hardly reached her familiar valerian-gathering place in the shore-meadow when she suddenly finds she is lost. Yes, and then it begins. First she finds herself in some dense thicket, goes in and cannot find her way out. Then she falls into a freshly dug ditch at the edge of the thicket and finds there a pair of brand-new crutches. But the crutches are in themselves a bad enough sign. Thirdly, everywhere, both the shore meadow and the thicket as well as this ditch, is full of all kinds of birds. There are crows, there are sparrows, there are unfamiliar birds with red breasts and yellow tails, there are sturdy-legged birds, there are birds with convex beaks. One particular bird is long and striped, like a cravat; it walks on two legs and croaks. Another is fat and round as a watermelon, but its eyes are terrible, the eyes of a tiger. It could be an owl. But what kind of bird the cravat-like one was, that is certainly unknown. And all those birds just went on jumping around, just went on jumping around, to and fro. All of them were on foot.

Seeing this, Aunt Olga stood where she was, and went on standing until she could no longer stand. Following the birds, Aunt Olga said to herself, remember now, Olga, everything you see, now something is going to happen, the return of the Stalin period or whatever, but nothing will stay the same. In Stalin's time the birds also went on foot; they could no longer be bothered to fly as they had eaten themselves full, because the harvests were always left ungathered.

In this way, with significant pauses, Aunt Olga gradually approaches Dostoyevsky's dream, but it remains unrecounted. That dream she never hears in Aunt Olga's version. Decades later, reading: 'In the eastern sky there hung a full moon. The moon fragmented into three pieces and those three pieces recombined. Then from inside the moon there emerged a shield on which was written, in church Slavonic, *Da! Da!* Those words moved over the entire sky from East to West and illuminated their way,' she will never know whether this was the same Dostoyevsky's dream, or another. Aunt Olga's story is interrupted by the clatter of the doorbell and replaced by it. The clatter of the bell is sharp as a razor and surprising as a slash-wound.

Aunt Olga does not even move. She sits as she was sitting. But Kinski the dog pads nervously from the kitchen to the hall and the hall to the kitchen. Its claws scratch and the whites of its eyes glisten. Aunt Olga whispers, 'Kinski, no!' It sounds like Chinese, it is true, but is nevertheless effective: Kinski lies down, looking guilty, and does not move. Now nothing more is to be heard. Whoever was at the door is completely convinced that there is no one at home, and goes away. Now the bell should ring no longer. But it does ring. And rings again.

Aunt Olga closes her eyes. Perhaps Aunt Olga is now invisible. But she, unlike Aunt Olga, is completely visible, pressing her rib-cage painfully against the table. Just now, Aunt Olga lifted a few eggs out of her shopping bag together with the bunch of grapes. They are still on the table, and quiver each time her heart beats. A few black flakes of soot have fallen on to their white shells.

6

From now on, she reacts coolly to the ringing of the doorbell. She has gathered courage. She is even a little disappointed that the door still stands in its place and has not been kicked in. From time to time, however, she creeps up to the door, presses her ear against the dark brown wood and listens. She has never yet heard anything interesting in the stairwell. Only a cat mewing, old women muttering and children chattering.

On the kitchen table is a saucer and on the saucer her salvation – the key to the security lock, which Aunt Olga put there ceremoniously before her departure. Underneath the saucer a piece of squared paper from a notebook has been left – a list of meals which Aunt Olga has put in the refrigerator with her own hands, and which are to be eaten in order of importance.

The most important, or number one, is half a browned chicken. Immediately after the chicken comes a packet of curd cheese, which can be eaten with either cherry sauce or honey, as one pleases. Because Aunt Olga has been anxious as to whether she will be understood correctly she has, to make certain, provided a plan drawing of the inside of the refrigerator. The clumsy drawing recalls the cross-section of a combustion engine. The foods which will spoil particularly easily are marked on the drawing with numbers indicated with thick arrows. The pears, for example, are marked with the number five, and are therefore not to be taken too seriously. The eggs and butter, on the other hand, are completely lacking in numbers.

As may be guessed, she starts with the pears, casting the chicken and the curd cheese a mischievous glance. Her pear-eating is not interrupted even by the ringing of the doorbell. Cold-bloodedly, she waits for a couple of moments; and, when the ringing is not renewed, goes and looks down at the courtyard through a gap in the curtains. No one is to be seen, with the exception of an old woman with a man's hat, who looks like the caretaker or the postwoman and is just stepping out of the main door.

Much more than the aggressive clatter of the doorbell, she would be startled by the quiet opening of the door and Father's reappearance; which would, of course, be entirely possible. Now she has also thoroughly examined the third room. Father is certainly not there, unless in ghostly form. In the third room, Father is not even behind the curtain; she has also inspected all the spaces behind the curtains. As she slouches from one room to another, her attention is attracted in increasing measure to one single object – the key, which rests on the white saucer, fish-like, although it does not look like a fish, but like a fish-shaped spinner. If she wished, she could put that magic piece of metal in her pocket, slam the door insolently behind her and disappear, without burning her bridges or severing her way back in all four compass directions. She could come back at any moment at all and no one would know where she had really been, whether hanging around the ticket booths at the railway station or reading the timetables on the wall of the bus station.

But instead she leafs through Lion's notebook and makes the acquaintance of his penknife. She realises that a small scout saw is concealed within the handle of the knife, and she cannot resist trying the dullness of the saw against pencils. In this work she ruins many good Faber pencils.

However she tries to fritter away her time, there is just one question in her head: has Leo yet telephoned *where he should*, and can the magic words 'unfit for permanent service in time of peace' already have been stamped in his passport? Beyond that, she cannot yet think of anything.

Aunt Olga has promised to come and tell her as soon as Lion has telephoned from Moscow and said how it has gone. If things have gone well, Lion will say that he succeeded in buying Mother those blue cups. But if things have gone badly (something for which one must also be prepared), he will announce curtly that he could not find the blue cups in Moscow and that it would be better for Mother to come herself.

Everything is clearer than clear and simpler than simple. One must just have more patience. Even if something feels confusing, one must simply stick with it and everything needful will become clear in time. Time – that she has too much of. In the living room, she has already peeped into all the drawers that are not locked. Concerning the content of the locked drawers, she has developed hypotheses and suspicions that do not bear criticism. So it is not worth repeating them. Of course she is unable to imagine the true contents of the locked drawers, among which there are even silver objects – Grandfather's paperknife and the case for the Torah, both of which are uncleaned and black as iron.

One of the locked drawers is completely filled with a mysterious box containing fragments of glass. This box must not be touched by a stranger's hand or seen by a stranger's eye. In the box are sombre and sparkling fragments of all the wine-glasses which *the bridegroom has crushed under his heel as a mark of the fragility of human life*, for four generations. All those goblet-smashing bridegrooms died long ago.

The unlocked drawers, fortunately, do not reveal anything so sacred. In them, she finds only black envelopes with old photographs and entire bundles of letters in German, Russian and English, as well as all kinds of incidentals – bookmarks, keys with and without rings, nail file, stamps and pre-war travel guides. Unsuspectingly, she leafs through a number of forbidden books and opens with a click a black case containing a pair of compasses, whose velvet interior does not conceal compasses but a very strong sleeping draught whose existence has long since been forgotten.

Growing bored with the drawers, she goes straight to the bathroom and seeks again from the cupboard the dark red towelling bag that contains the already familiar plait of hair. This time she tries the hair against her own head in the mirror and enjoys in full measure the sense of fear that is kindled for no reason at all as she unplaits the hair in the strained silence of the apartment. When the strange hair undulates down her back, it radiates a strange *sweetness of fear*. Looking at her, one could almost believe the claim of those who know about these things that the beauty of weapons and the rules of manhunts originate nowhere else but in the human heart. But she secretly enjoys the *sweetness of fear* as much as any swindler; she would like to repeat the experience as soon as the opportunity arises.

There will certainly be plenty of opportunities in the future. Let alone the present. As already mentioned, she can see all the events and places of the future through the sweetness of the fear of 1968. Her memory is like a door through which anyone can appear – a plain-clothes man, a man in uniform or a strange man accompanied by a white monkey.

Thus she sets the Riga bathroom aside for a moment and allows the stream to carry her to a Polish square filled with red evening sun in 1972. Pigeons babble, children climb on the wide, wet sides of the fountain. On the same well-sides sit a few boys who look like girls and girls who look like boys, whose gender can be determined infallibly only with reference to the size of their feet. The boys' feet are bigger, and no one can argue otherwise.

Heat rises from the cobbles of the square; the entire square glows. She sits between the children and the hippies and pushes her arms, with enjoyment, into the cloudy, surprisingly cold water. Pigeon-feathers, paper boats, foam and cigarette ends float on the surface of the water. Below, on the bottom, gleams a layer of coins. Time jerks forward and back so that one can do everything that is necessary.

The water laps. The hippies smile mysteriously, eat sausage and play the parts of dissolute angels. Their daisies and headbands belong to the kingdom of illusion rather than that of this calendar year.

For some time she gazes at the shimmer of the evening and the August moon, watches time as it moves forward and then backward; then she rises decisively and, prosaically, exits left.

This evening is followed by a long day in a previously unfamiliar part of the country. The windows of the bus do not open; black coal-dust penetrates through the ventilator in the roof. The grass is parched, the leaves of the trees brown. Corn is cut with a scythe. The old Polish women have on their heads ominous black cloths and wear half-coats, tied at the waist, with pleated hems, and nothing of the kind has been seen before or since. The wind murmurs. The fields and clearings are like large battlegrounds; even the clouds above these battlegrounds are like the blue official envelopes which can contain a death notice.

The Estonians do not want to go to Auschwitz. They curse in whispers: 'Why don't they show us the camps in Siberia!' Everyone in this bus could immediately tell a number of true stories about the Siberian death camps; these stories have been passed on from father to son and mother to daughter by mouth, like charms to cure snakebite or curses for iron.

Grumbling, they finally reach their destination, climb unenthusiastically out of the bus, hitch up their trousers and smooth their hair. Their attention is drawn to the lemonade kiosk, and they attack it immediately. Poison-red and TNT-yellow liquids fizz and splatter foam and sparks on to faces. This coloured water could equally well be drunk in a thousand other places, but only here can one look over the rim of one's paper cup at the rusted railway tracks and wooden surveillance towers that everyone has seen in pictures.

Dusty buses stand in rows in the square. Beside them are residential buildings. Sunflowers and dahlias blossom in the gardens, babies' bloomers dry on washing lines, cats sit on balconies washing their faces. A man is painting his fence. The view is ordinary, modest and idyllic.

Then they walk through the famous but, in reality, rather small and seemingly insignificant 'Arbeit macht frei' gate and are *inside*. *Inside*, everything looks like the inside of any country school on the first day of term. People holding bunches of gladioli and clearing their throats shift their feet on the spot like embarrassed parents on the red, gravel-strewn pathways between the low, reticent brick buildings. The ceremony is either about to begin or else it has just ended. Only the white-socked schoolchildren are missing.

People wipe their sweat away and look around them. Some weep, others laugh. The weeping and the laughter give rise to a strange hubbub. Now the voices of the Estonians are heard. The ones standing further back ask the ones further forward: 'Have you seen the hair yet? Where's the *hair*?'

In the end, even those at the very back get to see the famous pile of hair. The faded, dusty and tangled hair is a disappointment to everybody. Here, close to the hair, boots, spectacles, toothbrushes and mugs have also been put on show. Spectacle lenses glint mockingly as if they knew something completely new and particular about hell and cabaret,* human hearts and the teachings of religions.

Everything is explained by a small, dark woman, a former prisoner. Cheerfully and vividly she tells the story of the thousand women who were given just one bucket of water a day for both washing and drinking. It is just as if she were telling a story which always begins in the same way: 'Es war einmal... Zili byli... Once upon a time...'

The former prisoner belongs to the camp heart and soul; she is the camp's veteran and *patriot*. The visitors eye her bare legs and arms with open interest, seeking wounds and whip-lash marks, and they are deeply disappointed not to find them. In order to make a bigger impression on them, she should have bones, instead of feet, stuffed into her shoes.

The Estonian group leader asks, for form's sake: 'Tell us, please, why you were taken to the camp.' The woman answers with pleasure: 'My husband's name was Joseph and mine is Mary. They asked whether it was Jesus I intended to give birth to and look – they put me in the camp.'

'Too neat to be true,' some listeners voice their suspicions, but others keep them under control. The woman looks at both with all-seeing and maternal eyes.

They go through the personal papers, Jewish stars and death

warrants and back into the courtyard. The woman's thoroughgoing explanation makes the group restless. The entire camp feels, to the Estonians, small and ornamental. There are no gold-mines, no deserted *taiga* or unburied bodies lying just behind the village. Nothing with any connection to the Estonians' idea of a proper camp and camp life. Provocatively, they hack away at the plaster on the wall of the building where experiments were carried out on pregnant women. Everyone feels hot; sweat flows. For this reason they lend only half an ear to reminiscences and observations about the gas chambers, the *Kapos** and the doctor who was called the Angel of Death.

Still left are the *chambers and ovens*. They march quickly through the chambers; their cracked concrete floors and empty clothes-hooks are unable to make any kind of impression. Finally they arrive at the *ovens*. Everyone notices that something black and oily has run out of the oven mouth. Someone asks: 'Have these ovens been *washed*?'

At last they reach the bus again. But there it becomes clear that on the dusty side of the bus, right under the Sovtrasovto trademark, a slogan has been written in Polish which, examined and explained more closely, turns out to be the question: 'Do you remember 1968?', which is followed by the incomprehensible threat, 'Go home, murderers!'

Once again the Estonians divide into impassioned groups, and some argue: 'But we're *Estonians*! We haven't done anything!', while others, more slow-witted, are amazed: 'What devils! Just look at what they dare say!', and a secret *Schadenfreude* is audible in their voices.

As they reach the hotel, the wind has risen and the glass doors of the hotel crackle unpleasantly. They take the lift up to their rooms, which have bare, office-green walls and chilly, sad ceiling lamps. The rainwater is already trickling down the window panes; the raw lamplight dims the still rawer lightning. The wind rattles the badly closed windows. At the ends of the beds lie open suitcases; clothes are strewn on the chairs. From the corridor behind the thin door, the corridor of Poland, indistinct speech is audible, and dragging footsteps. The long office corridor is perhaps at this moment being traversed by a mute line of people, all of them wearing thick coats and with suitcases in their hands. The queue sways and mutters; it rises up from the depths of time and sinks down to the depths of time.

The rain on the other side of the window glimmers from time to time, lit up sombrely by the lightning, and every bolt of lightning in the Polish sky brings to mind the German name, 'Schicksal'.

But this is nothing yet compared to the future and to Bucharest, where small Pioneers, their ribs showing individually through their shirt-fabric, carry on their lips the frightening name of their dictator day and night, on the radio and on television, in squares and on speakers' platforms. Where every dearly acquired piece of meat bears the taste of *sacrificial meat*. Where sugar-backed maggots climb out of the dessert bowls of an expensive restaurant. Where anyone at all can receive laundry and also lose his notebook and his exposed film, if he has been naïve enough to make notes and take photographs. Where, as early as 1941, the bodies of Jews are seen in butchers' shops hanging in place of animal carcasses.

But what is this compared to New York, where the wind drives back and forth in front of the Plaza Hotel a bin liner whose black, shiny surface is, it seems, as if made for the Angel of the Lord to write a few notes about the end of the world. It is very possible that he has noted down the answer to the question of why Kafka's house in Prague shook when Brezhnev's tanks arrived and why the gravestones in the old Jewish cemetery trembled and rose from the ground by themselves.

Perhaps the Angel of the Lord will also answer, on the New York rubbish bag, the question of why the tragic is always comical and why the cry for help of the famous dramatists, poets and writers concerning the bloodbath of the Prague curfew, a cry which no one hears, decides the future of many peoples, perhaps even that of the entire world.

Perhaps a couple of words have also been noted on the bin liner concerning the thick black smoke which rises from the windows which are broken in Harlem for amusement's sake, floats as far as Central Park and turns everything created by human hand into matter condemned to the rubbish tip, and makes the charm of objects empty, cursed and pathetic. The giant city spreads its black, rustling plastic wings and their shadow is like the shadow of the future. It reaches places it should not, according to common sense, be able to reach. It reaches back to the past, to the city of Riga and the glow of an early autumn sunset in 1968, which can be seen from the west window.

That bleak and ebbing row of lights forces her to become, once again, the prisoner of the present year. However she may play, may spread the strange hair in front of her face, the moment will nevertheless still arrive when restlessness will force her to look at the clock, and then an expression will be seen on her young face which is as old as the whole world. Perhaps it is the expression of one who waits, or perhaps it is one whose significance will become clear only in the future.

The cold wind makes the black waters sway. The big fish at the bottom of the Daugava river is already asleep, its nose under a sunken log. Toward night, the wind continues to strengthen; in gardens, it breaks the branches of apple trees and hurls as yet unripe apples to the ground. The darkness of the cities is illuminated by the words MEAT and CINEMA, written in neon. In the doorways and in the shadows of the kiosks, glowing cigarette-ends force late home-goers to quicken their steps.

Garrisons, military areas, potato fields and children's sandpits move along their agreed routes toward the end-point of history. She who, holding her breath, listens to the darkness, can this evening easily sense the mineral, vegetable and animal kingdoms moaning in the human language.

The cold, ebbing light draws strange letters on the walls of the room which, minute by minute, become more obscure and finally disappear completely, melt into the wallpaper and will not re-appear in precisely the same form until a year later. When the time of day and the season allow again. When the cycle is complete.

On the kitchen table it is still possible to see the white saucer, but the key on it can no longer be made out by the naked eye. She returns in her thoughts to that key again and again, and anyone who followed her expression could easily believe that her *perspectiveless language* does, after all, contain the word 'love', like all other languages, and that it is precisely this word that she is currently using in her thoughts. The more high-flown and emotional the words she chooses, the more difficult it is for her to apprehend their use. The prouder and more indefinite her uncertainty-repelling shoulder-shrugs.

She expertly opens the first book she encounters and looks in it for omens and clues. This time her finger lands on a line so well-known to theatre people: 'Ivanov (*laughing*): Not a wedding but a parliamentary debate! Bravo, bravo!...', which is followed by a still more famous line: 'Ivanov: Leave me alone!' *Runs to one side and shoots himself. Curtain.*

This hint or clue from Chekhov calls to her lips a peculiar new kind of smile which could be described accurately only by replacing one well-worn word with another. The word 'tender' with the word 'enigmatic', or vice versa. Despite its tenderness, this smile is not warm or particularly adult. This smile is as cold as March, as wavering and windy, originating from the air rather than the earth. The threat it conceals, too, belongs to a strange climate.

That smile is now reflected, even in the darkness of the evening, in the dented silver tray on the table, with which the *Red Guard* amused itself on Aunt Olga's tenth birthday. Aunt Olga was supposed to slide down a hill with the tray as her sledge. Not once or twice, but as many as twenty times, and not in a dress, but with her blue bottom quite bare. The Red Guard shouted happily: 'Hey, Sarah! Faster!', and threw burning pieces of newspaper on to the ice in encouragement until at the bottom of the slope an angry officer who, for some reason, gave her back the silver tray, snapped: 'On your way, then!'

For her, the silver tray and its dubious past do not say anything; neither do the paw-legged chairs, which come from the late

Grandfather's house and which, in Lion's childhood imaginings, gathered together to goose-step in a line through forests and over mountains, seeking, through lands and countries, Grandfather's grave, to grieve by. Only when they reached the Atlantic Ocean did they turn back and return via Warsaw to Riga. All the love and sorrow associated with these objects now fill the entire dark, silent room.

In order to break the silence, she flops on her stomach on to the sofa, but stops to listen and gradually tenses like a tautened string. Something happens which simultaneously takes from her all her attention, her power and her energy. Her wrists seem to narrow visibly, her cheekbones become gentler and her eyelashes sharper. She *waits. Tastes of the goblet of expectation*, like the blessed Genevieve.

Radios crackle, newspapers are being typeset, the conscripts' hair has already been shaved and thrown into the rubbish bin. The arms of those who resist are twisted behind their backs. Crew-cut, the boys grind their teeth and believe that the only symbol of freedom is the fact that you have not had your head shaved. The basis for the choked tears of the conscripts is removed by the fact of how quickly human hair grows compared to the slow growth of the freedom of the world.

The wind always howls and whines in the background of historical events; now, too, it is present; under the shelter of night it throws sand in the eyes of Czech writers so that they must rub their eyes with their fists, and this makes them seem helpless and childish. But the Angel of the Lord rushes unnoticed behind their backs, and writes in the chilly, undulating air above the shores of the Baltic: 'Flee, child of freedom, give shelter to the freedom of the world.' At this point the angel's hand pauses, he sinks into thought, but adds: 'Violence loves freedom, wants to conquer it and subdue it to its power...' and waits, with great interest, to see when a poet from a former small Baltic country (whose hair is comparatively long and whose radio is so broken that he can hear nothing of the stations of the free West but mere ominous crackling) will find these lines in the air and write them on paper.

This text will flutter and undulate on these shores for a long time, living its own life.

But as she sits on the sofa at the same time in Riga, she presses the palms of her hand between her knees, holds her breath and demands an end to her waiting. Demands it with such strength that she begins to feel dizzy and there are sparks in her eyes. What do the stubs of manuscripts mean to her, or the inviolability of state boundaries? She does not hear or see, does not feel compassion or pity. The way in which, under her worn dressing gown, she curls up and puts her hands to her neck to warm could be moving if it were not for the fact that everyone who waits has always done so. The movements of her lips show that she is repeating the same familiar prayer, whose customary and classical beginning: 'Dear God, grant that...' ends with grey official language, that they will write 'Unfit for permanent service in time of peace'.

In the name of accuracy, it should be said that similar awkward prayers are rising today by the thousand, whole flocks of them, into the night sky of eastern Europe. They drift over cranes, telephone wires and sandpits like sheets of paper torn out of personal files. Where they disappear to, who takes charge of them, not a living soul can know.

The tinkle of the telephone is audible from beneath the pile of cushions, dark as the depths of the earth. She listens. Raises her head. Mistakes the smothered tinkling for the ringing of the doorbell. It is a little while before realises she should look in the direction of the telephone. The order not to answer the telephone has already penetrated her skull, but despite it the tinkling of the phone attracts her like a magnet. Nevertheless, it should be as clear to her as a multiplication table: no one will call *her* in this apartment. But because her multiplication tables are not so well-lodged in her brain that she could tell you in her sleep what seven eights are, she steps up to the telephone, pushes the cushions on to the floor and picks up, or rather grabs, the receiver.

As already mentioned, the entire apartment is filled with a dense, almost visible silence. Even the dripping of the tap is no longer to be heard. The magical humming that comes from the black telephone receiver is all the more audible.

Suddenly the humming is severed, and a perfectly ordinary, bellicose woman's voices hisses in clear Russian: 'Speak!' She holds the receiver more closely to her ear. Its edge presses against her ear like the barrel of a revolver. Then she hears, in the receiver, breathing, not realising that her own breaths, too, can be heard clearly. Now the telephone receiver no longer recalls a weapon but a living, hot mouth pressed against her ear. Her mouth says not a word. It obeys the interdiction.

Then there is a click, the voice of the breathing is cut off, and all that is left is a lifeless buzzing. In the dark, the water of the Moscow river glimmers dimly like a silken cravat from tsarist times. Lion stands in the street in front of the telegraph office, gathers himself together and then disappears underground, into a tunnel. The big city above ground merely murmurs, calls and wallows in soot and dust. All its telephone kiosks, food shops and offices creep in jerks toward tomorrow, they are *on the way to the future*, as the slogans on the walls of the buildings announce. Dzerzhinsky Square moves jerkily toward the future, too, with its eponymous statue, which is as black and heavy as a machine part.

The prosaic, cellophane-covered plates of sausage and ham on the Kremlin's buffet tables move forward in the flashing river of time. For a moment the river casts the Kremlin's plates of sandwiches on to the shore, and immediately afterward a random participant in a Writers' Congress from beyond the Urals stretches out her hand toward them; as she fishes for the sandwiches in the river of time, a desperate and humble gleam appears in her eyes. It is her intention to buy a larger number of these sandwiches to take with her. Not to eat on the spot in the Kremlin but to take home, as she wants her husband and her two daughters too, in their industrial city on the far side of the Urals, to have their share of the sacrament of the Kremlin.

The waiter, who has also, with the entire Kremlin, been washed into the river of time for a moment, refuses to sell the sandwiches to anyone. For some reason this congress participant's face does not please the waiter at all. The participant grows heated, begins

91

to puff and blow; her briefcase falls and opens, out roll oranges, on to the floor spread boxes of tights; the devil knows what happens.

The other congress participants gather in a group at the doors, they adjust their ties and rock their weight from their heels to their toes and back again, smiling sleepily and maliciously. All the participants are as dark and heavy as Dzerzhinsky's statue or an iron filing cabinet in which money and secret circular letters are stored. The smell of newsprint and Armenian cognac rises from the participants, and this joins battle with the scent of chlorine in the corridors, scarcely detectable but all the more desolate for that.

Some experienced congress participants who have visited the buffet tables of the Kremlin more than once notice on the counter a hot mushroom dish; its name is the strange and incomprehensible 'Julienne'. Pressing their ties against their chests as they walk, the participants rush toward 'Julienne' and disappear from view, for the river of time takes it with them, together with the echoing, colonnaded rooms. Lenin's mausoleum, too, jerks and shudders as if the dead man were trying to get out from under the glass, to escape and to hide.

Behind Lion's back, in the escalator that descends deep into the bowels of the earth, stand two men in string vests, telling each other jokes, turn and turn about. The names of the characters in the jokes are Sarah and Abraham. In the men's string bags watermelons bounce to the rhythm of their laughter; on seeing them, anyone at all would swallow.

The telephone receiver has left the red mark of a hot mouth on Lion's temple and earlobe, which he does not even realise he should cover. Down in the tunnel there howls an underground black wind. Against the flesh-coloured marble walls of the metro's public secret corridors the threat rebounds: 'Caution. Doors closing.'

7

The power of the nights grows. It happens soundlessly, as if incidentally, of itself, at the expense of the days. It is not therefore worth wondering, vainly, why the days keep growing shorter but the nights, on the other hand, continue to grow longer and longer.

Whether few or many days and nights have passed, no one knows; on this question it is hard for even nations and states to reach agreement, let alone *private individuals*. TASS makes announcements more often and in ever more ceremonial terms about the *unprecedented flowering* of culture and economics which the *working people* of Czechoslovakia have unexpectedly achieved during the course of August.

From time to time she hears these ceremonial announcements through the open ventilation window on the radio downstairs. But she allows such information to pass wantonly in through one ear and out through the other, because despising all kinds of political statements has been, until now, as self-evident a business as breathing to her and others like her. If one wishes to serve the word and colour and the freedom of the world, one must not allow *the lies of the mass media to blind one*.

Infatuated by this vain and underhand slogan, she has never yet, during these days, switched on the radio or the television. Quite the reverse – she lets these instruments feel the full force of her disdain. She allows a thick layer of dust to gather on the screen and piles heavy art books around the radio; at night, she drags them to the sofa, too, and leafs through them until dawn, gnawing at the treats bought by Aunt Olga – dried black plums, raisins and figs. When the moon sets and the first trams are already on the move, she throws her last enquiring glances at the mirrors, the

93

doors and the curtains, switches off the lamp and sleeps sweetly; ranged around her are Venuses, opening shells, black squares, burning giraffes and thick sofa-cushions, and prune stones and apple cores press her side.

She is found in this condition by Aunt Olga who, a bad sleeper, is up early and simply cannot wait for night finally to turn to day. Moreover, today she has fresh news. Now she is here, naturally accompanied by Kinski the dog, and sets to work at once. The sleeper is awakened, and while she is performing her ablutions Aunt Olga has already wiped the floors with a damp cloth. Dusting is in progress. Meanwhile, Aunt Olga is amicably dispensing advice. She has many memories and comments about cleaning. She compares the old dusters, made of cockerel-feathers, to today's scraps of flannel, and the pre-war chicken's wings to today's floor brushes, and as a result she does not immediately convey the news which is awaited with burning eyes.

Finally Aunt Olga's cleaning routine reaches the clay box. Now she sets down the duster, takes the familiar long-spouted watering can from behind the curtain and waters the clay in the box thoroughly, expertly and with care. This activity is accompanied by humming, in which both reproaches and hope can be heard: 'Well, now the clay's been dampened. Let him come, as soon as he likes, and set to work! What does this mean, now! Rush off, would you, leave the clay to dry, Aunt Olga will come and dampen it, to be sure! I suppose you think you're some great master, so mature that you don't need to work, everything just comes of itself. But it doesn't! And the bronze-founder has already rung to ask where the new piece is. Now he'll take that Ukrainian on to do the job. It's the same to him, after all, as long as the foundry goes on working.'

Muttering, Aunt Olga pulls the roller blinds straight and sets the cushions and books in their correct places. Only afterwards does she pause solemnly in her activities, and brings to the table in the living room a strange vase showing a dragon swallowing a clock face; in it a bunch of heather has been placed. Aunt Olga herself gathered the heather from the roots of a stand of spruces on her journey here on an early-morning train. From the purple flowers rises the scent of heath-sand and bees, the severity of the empty sky, which gives Aunt Olga's brief, ordinary words a different colour from what they might otherwise have.

That fistful of seaside heather increases her heart-rate much more than Aunt Olga's words, which she does not, in any case, completely understand. Where now are last week's heather moors, the campfire on the sand and the merging shadows! She listens to Aunt Olga's news with only half an ear. Although there is reason to listen.

Yes – Lion telephoned last night from Moscow and said as follows: he might have an opportunity to *buy these blue cups* (here Aunt Olga interrupts herself and asks in her piercing class-teacher's voice: 'Well, why did he go to Moscow?' and nods when she receives the correct answer: 'To buy blue cups'), the entire dinner service in fact, but he cannot make such a large purchase alone without discussing it with the others. The news was perfectly good, but incomprehensible. What does *dinner service* mean? Lion's voice on the telephone was sombre. Very sombre. After the conversation, Mother was quite *out of her mind*; she rushed through the room, stubbornly repeating just three phrases: 'Don't come to me! I'm the mother! And I didn't *like* his voice!' Mother leaves the iron switched on, by mistake, for almost three hours, without anyone realising. It was only because of Father that common sense prevailed in the house. If Father had not been there, who knows what could have happened. Father has already begun to *take measures*. This Aunt Olga emphasises, looking particularly mysterious and satisfied. What measures they are is not known. In any case both of them, Father and Mother, travelled, as soon as the opportunity arose, to meet their son in Moscow. When Father will fly back to his pretty little canton of Thurgau Aunt Olga does not say.

In general, however, Aunt Olga's story sounds rather dry and dull. It is as if there is news and there is not. But perhaps Aunt Olga has not been privy to everything that is planned. Certainly not as much as Kinski the dog, who has been present in person during every conversation between Mother and Father, in the secret whirlpool of events. This time, Kinski looks more like a plain-clothes man than a director, although the similarity may be merely coincidental. But it is not worth forgetting that Aunt Olga's guiding principle has always been 'Hope', and that even now she remains faithful as she sinks heavily to her knees and whispers into Kinski's smooth, brown ear: 'Kinski, where's Lion! Seek!' In this way it is as if Aunt Olga has switched on some extraordinary device inside Kinski. Kinski sniffs busily, not leaving a single corner uninspected, through the whole apartment, and strangely enough – finally points to the clay box. He even wags his tail. For Kinski wishes to say that it is not completely in vain that Lion has worked so much with that clay. If he has not achieved anything else, then he has at least succeeded in leaving the scent of his own blood on it.

When the inevitable tea-drinking ritual has been completed and the contents of the refrigerator inspected and, through Aunt Olga's offices, generously refilled, the moment arrives when Aunt Olga puts her coat on again and clips the lead to Kinski's neck.

After Aunt Olga's departure, the apartment is as empty as a winter's night. The rooms are very high, the door is very firmly closed, the curtains very thick. She throws one of the many sofa cushions on to the floor, pushes her freezing bare toe under the cushion and writes two long letters, her back straight, the light coming from the left, without further thought; she folds them up without reading them. She strokes the paper with her hand as if it were human skin. Is lost in thought, allows sentences without beginnings or endings to arise in her mind, fragments of famous, much-recited autumnal melancholia, which she eyes from every side and compares curiously and dreamily to her own.

Then she crumples up the letters she has written and throws them with surprising skill behind the sofa. She can do nothing else with them, for even if she wanted to, she could not send them to Tallinn, as she does not know her closest friends' postal addresses, let alone their telephone numbers. It has simply not occurred to her that they might have addresses. Until now, she has known that

Heller lives in the Second-House-After-The-Pharmacy, Matsson lives Behind-The-Church, First-Stairway-Third-Floor, but Linde, on the other hand, lives Above-The-Dry-Cleaner.

Even she understands that such directions and clues are not written in the space for the address on envelopes. And better so! What kind of letters are they, after all! If they had mentioned, in even half a word, the silence that follows the ringing of the doorbell! If they had, even in passing, dealt with the buzzing of the electric lamp at midnight! Ah, if there had been just one hint of the Kalashnikov assault rifle or even of the garrison staff. But she does not even know the weapons' name! She is not au fait with life as it is lived! She just sits within four walls. Does not listen to the radio, does not read the newspaper. She has just one privilege, which no one can deny her – for no other creature can fill the place in the sea of air which she fills with her own body. Pondering this now, she feels as if everyone else has long been certain of how life is to be lived, they have ferreted from somewhere all the rules and formulae and do not wonder at anything any more in the way that she does.

But morning becomes noon, the light makes its journey, the colour of the air changes and with it landscapes, street vistas and objects in the room. The wind begins to blow; from time to time its howling even obscures the noise of the traffic. From below in the yard, a woman's clear laugh and the babbling of a baby can be heard. The glittering eye of a brightly coloured pigeon looks in through the window, as demanding as if the bird were delivering a letter.

From the crack in the curtain, the hard and smooth blue vault of the sky can be seen, and beneath it the city of Riga which, together with the river Daugava, the big fish, the Latvian stories, the courtyard and the baby babbling in the courtyard, has already set off and is moving ever faster away, toward the end of the century, a shiveringly cold winter's night when blood splashes, bones crumple, life is a dream and everyone who does not yet know will soon find out what a Kalashnikov assault rifle is. When, in the midst of the shouting and the hubbub, flaming with smoke,

97

barricades and shards of glass, a strange man shuffles along with his white monkey, offering the sweetness of fear and the beauty of weapons.

Before the sun reaches the kitchen window and the time is one, everything in the future has already been decided, the number of deciding factors being three – the first is the door that must not be opened, the second the window that must not be looked out of, and the third the telephone that must not be spoken into. Where this trio coincides, something will happen, sooner or later. 'Violence,' cries the western radio station in passing, and then falls silent, wheezing. 'Better a *verst* wrong than a span wrong,' says the Angel of the Lord to the city of Riga, but in his mouth that old proverb is transformed into an inflammatory speech which echoes hollowly through the clanking of the tram, the sighing of the wind and the double glazing.

She stretches, reaches out her hand and then takes from the bowl a large, white apple which has spent this summer hanging from a tree-branch near the Latvian and Estonian border and sucked itself full of the fire, water and shadows of summer, the realism of cow-manure and the pathos of the starry sky, and been transformed into a fruit that is touched by time and space and melts in the mouth.

It is the apple about which, twenty-two years later, she is told by the flaxen-haired Maarja, who has written 280 pages about Estonian life and death in Swedish; a dead person's apple. The NKVD killed her father in 1944. In a building which still stands and which Maarja has been shown, in Estonia. Apparently a dull and ordinary building, not at all like the scene of a murder; food had been made in the kitchen and a television set had stood in the corner. But behind the house in the garden grew a gnarled old apple tree; it had big, white apples that glowed like the moon.

Underneath this apple tree was a piece of earth where time stops. The stopping of time could apparently be seen immediately and even with the naked eye. It does not rain there, and if someone says something, it cannot be heard.

On the same piece of earth Maarja, the dead person's daughter, had found a white apple and put it, without further thought, into her coat pocket, not even herself knowing why. When she took the apple out of her pocket that evening, it became clear what it was. Information. The message which did not come when the little daughter waited, her feet freezing, secretly, for her own dead father at the edge of the great Swedish snowfield.

It must be said that the same black spark glows in the eyes of both narrator and listener; it reveals history in quite a different light, and as they notice this the Swedes fall silent and eye the speakers enquiringly and with excitement. As the speakers notice this, they exchange glances and burst out laughing. The summer café buzzes, a gentle wind stirs the hair; who could believe that about 350 kilometres east of Stockholm, on the other side of the sea, there grows a tree under which time has stopped. 'Yes indeed, who would believe it?' the speakers assure their audience enthusiastically, with one voice; their own enthusiasm amuses them, and they cannot restrain their laughter. But there is nothing to laugh at here. The father of one of them has been killed and the other has a Soviet passport in her pocket. So it is, and they feel like laughing, and that is what differentiates them from the Swedes.

And although there is still a long time to that debate, half a lifetime, she is preparing for it this very day. Why otherwise would she look at the large white summer apple in her hand with such excitement, as if she really believed that it was possible to squeeze time and space into it, or at least Estonia's Years of Destiny.

But outside the same wind of 1968 blows the leaves of the trees over and drives winds and swallows from north to south. At sea, the crests of waves must be breaking. It is to be feared that the sombre glint of the security-lock key on the white saucer will grasp hold of the entire day if the key is not put in a pocket. The time is almost half past twelve; teeth are sunk into the apple, a decision has been made.

For a moment her face regains its former carefree and arrogant expression, but the expression no longer sticks – neither her eyelids nor her mouth, neither her nose nor her cheeks, can retain it.

Nevertheless, it is precisely she who wishes, for example, to sleep through the night by act of will, to block her ears and wash her hands clean. She has not promised anything. She is quite sure that it is unnecessary to do anything but shrug her shoulders and leave anywhere where she is not comfortable – and all will be well. Plain-clothes men will disappear into the wind like smoke, the nightingale will be forgotten, the Angel of the Lord will close his notebook, there will be time for everything; let someone else taste from the cup of waiting.

Much more than the cup of waiting and the human heart, she is vexed by her own sandals, whose strap buckle she rattles with dissatisfaction. She has nothing else to put on her feet, although a piercing wind is blowing outside and no one goes barefoot any more. As she does up the dusty straps of her sandals, she recalls a morning in the Bible story, which she has always imagined in the same way: all the grass that has grown has burned; all that is left are thistles and wormwood. The wind that blows is so chill and the sun so bright that tears come unbidden to Abraham's eyes. The dust whirls and the logs piled behind Isaac's back for the sacrificial fire crackle so monotonously that the crackling, like love, cannot in any way be understood.

Then she is suddenly in a hurry; there is no more time to play with imaginings. It turns out that she has (and not just in her possession but by some miracle with her on the journey) a woollen jumper, rough and relaxed. It is true that it does not in the least correspond to her image of what a real jumper ought to look like. Naturally a real jumper should be *black*, not grey. *Suitably roomy*, not *baggy*. Nevertheless she pulls on this grey and baggy jumper as triumphantly as if it were black and suitably roomy.

Lion's beloved knife and his precious notebook she puts without further thought into her own pocket, and tries to whistle. Not very expertly; breathlessly and without any kind of tune.

She looks challengingly past the clay box and the sculptured shape wrapped in plastic film. At this moment she is almost sure that it is not in vain that Aunt Olga has spoiled her, and that she does not bring her apples and grapes merely on account of her pretty eyes. Perhaps Aunt Olga is merely following orders given by Father and simply doing what Father wants. But what does Father want?

Now she becomes confused and is no longer very sure of anything. Nevertheless she pulls herself together quickly, and at a stroke solves the problem of what Father wants.

Quite certainly, Father wishes his son to return home with good news. Everyone knows that he who goes away brings back home his own family's expectation. But not any old expectation; only an expectation of a certain kind, and the right kind. The kind that takes the eyes from the head and the words from the mouth. Both Father and Mother, and Aunt Olga too, have waited long enough in their lives; now their strength is at an end, and their waiting no longer has the proper capacity or power. So that she who *has* it will now meet a real need in this house. For her, fish is fried as for a cat, and the juiciest pears are chosen from the market as for someone who is dying. She must have seedless raisins and rare, red-fleshed peaches. She is sheltered like a speaking fish or a living statue, at home behind locked doors and heavy curtains.

And, strangely enough, she has begun to wait. If things go on like this, all that will be left of her on the sofa will be a grey, goat-butted woollen sweater, white bones and a heart melted to a lump.

In order to save what can still be saved, she grabs a handful of raisins and slips out through the door into the stairwell. The door behind her closes automatically. All that is heard is a quiet click.

Nothing happens. No one is to be seen. For a moment she is confused by her action; then she gets her wind back, gives her legs their marching orders and does not stop until she finds herself by a bench in a distant boulevard. And even then she stops only to count her money. She has just as little as before; no change has taken place in this respect, and she pushes the leathery, faded-looking notes carelessly back into her pocket. To her eyes, which have grown accustomed to the dimness of the apartment rooms, the light is at first too bright, but nevertheless she measures up buildings and people with a feral gaze, as if seeing them for the first time.

The people are wearing caps and scarves. Their mouths are locked and their eyes cast down to the ground. Most of them carry fat string bags full of cucumbers, potatoes and cabbages; visible in a few is a whole black and moist fishtail. Pieces of meat are wrapped in fragile white paper which absorbs bloodstains. A dozen eggs have been bought, and a litre or so of milk. Even those who have not bought anything, or do not apparently intend to do so, look around them and get in the way of the others.

There are, in general, a lot of people. The crowds people the tram and bus stops, giving rise to eddies and currents around the department stores. A rough glance gives the impression that people's clothes are dark and thick, as if everyone were wearing coarse wool jackets, fur caps and military boots. Closer examination, however, reveals that no one has yet put a fur hat on their head and that instead of coarse wool jackets they are wearing quite thin suits or frankly colourful dresses. The military boots, too, turn out, on closer inspection, to be quite ordinary walking shoes. So these people cannot, after all, be criticised for anything.

She does not, nevertheless, allow the human current to take her with it nearly as easily as one might suppose, but keeps her ears and eyes open constantly and tries to commit to memory landmarks with whose help she might find *her way back*.

Beside a wooden fence there stands a little boy with a hen. Around the thick yellow leg of the hen is tied a piece of string whose other end the child holds tightly in his hand. At that moment a random passer-by stops in front of the child, a little old lady, and asks: 'Is it yours, that hen?', to which the boy answers, briskly and with a military air: 'Mine!' The old lady begins to make a deal: 'Sell your hen to me. Stop teasing it. I'll take it home to Jurmala, let it eat and drink, and soon it'll start to lay eggs.' The boy squeezes his eyes tightly shut and shakes his ball-like, crew-cut head: 'I won't sell her! She's my playmate!'

The wooden fence, the little boy, the hen and the overheard conversation constitute a landmark with whose help she believes she will find her way back. Only, it is true, if the little boy is still standing there with his hen, and the boy and the old lady are still repeating those same words. In any case, she now has one landmark – the boy with his hen and the little old lady.

Another landmark which she similarly commits to memory belongs, unfortunately, to the same class. For the second landmark is a red comb which some one has lost in front of a baker's shop.

When she finally finds herself in front of the railway station, it cannot be said that this makes her particularly happy. She remains standing, undecided, her left hand screwed into a fist in her pocket. There she continues to warm the penknife whose red, smooth side has been completely ruined by scratching on it, in crooked and disproportionately large letters, LEV.

The square in front of the station is black with people; coarse wool jackets and fur hats come to mind once more. Greasy pies, cold boiled eggs, beer sausages and frankfurters are on sale from the kiosks. Everyone is eating. Sauce and fruit juice flow between some people's fingers, oil and fat between others'. Overfed pigeons peck; vigorous brown sparrows scamper between them. All the birds walk on foot. She notices that it is considerably safer outside among people than behind the locked door and curtained windows of the apartment. She mills around among the people for a little longer, inspects timetables and the length of ticket queues.

Then she has a ticket. Train number 188/187, Minsk-Vilnius-Riga-Tallinn. No one forces her to step into the carriage marked on the ticket or to sit down in the designated seat. No one can even know that she has bought a rail ticket. There is no reason for her to bite her lips or shift her feet.

There is a little less than an hour left until the train's departure. That hour she spends standing on the platform, following the movement of the hands of the clock. The loudspeakers crackle and make audible impassioned and hissing orders in Latvian and Russian. When, as if by magic, crowds of people weighed down by baggage emerge from the mouth of the tunnel at short intervals, they swarm up and down the platform for a while and then disappear without trace, again as if by magic. Engine-smoke and the bitter and harsh smell of iron hover in the air. A hunchbacked old man taps the wheels with an iron rod; from time to time he stops, jerks, cranes his long, thin neck and looks under the train as if he has seen a fat wallet or the body of Anna Karenina.

Why should the man with the iron bar be moved by the trembling of pale eyelids or the red of lips, let alone bare, cold and bluish anklebones?

The cycle of the clock hands is complete; the train sets off, on time, bringing shelter and warmth. That decides the matter.

8

If the journey from Riga to Tallinn lasts seven hours and if each hour has its own demon, which fights with that hour's own angel, much can happen in seven hours – noon can become evening; surveillance at state boundaries can be strengthened; new commands and advice can be issued by *a higher level*; daylight in the train carriage can unnoticeably become yellow barrack lighting; as darkness comes window panes can become completely black; and it is no wonder if the glimmering, transparent faces of the train passengers appear in them. The distances, which were long ago decided upon and transferred to all maps, are so enormous in scale that they cannot be understood by the intellect.

Before the train is even properly in motion, the city of Riga becomes an image and a memory; it becomes a threatening, mythical illusion which slowly and heavily sinks beneath the convexity of the Earth. Will the eyes of those who are now travelling away ever see this city again? Is it possible that their feet will step again on this same asphalt?

This thought does not either cool or warm her. She does not even bother to look out of the carriage window; she does not cast a single glance at the buildings of the suburb whose windows reflect an ardent and cold sky blue. She simply pulls her frozen fingers deep inside the sleeves of her jumper and pulls the woollen polo neck as far up as she can, to her ears if possible. Her bones are at this moment completely hollow inside. They are still full of the chilly draught of the platforms and tunnels, grey as asphalt and black as coal.

What she is currently thinking is very simple and very ordinary – a quilt and a pillow, gloves and socks. In fact, only a home-knitted shawl, a burning torch and a living lamb are missing!

She does not warm up until the train has reached Cesis; she begins to feel sleepy and rests her cheek against the rhythmically shaking little table underneath the window, and her faded, streaked hair falls over the table. She forces herself, however, to open her eyes from time to time, and surveys her immediate surroundings through her hair. She does not lose her vigilance. In her hand, in her fist, she holds, even half asleep, the key and the knife, as if they were a peculiar and great fortune whose value grows larger the farther the train travels from Riga.

The entire carriage seems dead. Half the seats are empty. Dust hovers in the sunlight in the corridor. But this is only a disappointing first impression. Closer inspection reveals that the luggage racks are full of luggage, the pegs of jackets and coats. But the owners of the things and coats themselves are sitting in the restaurant, drinking beer and liquor, smoking cigarettes and telling jokes against the state.

Two girls have appeared in the carriage. They take seats directly opposite her and begin enthusiastically and with all their hearts to survey their shopping. Hearing these girls speaking clear Estonian, she begins to follow them secretly.

Later it is already very difficult, if not impossible, to be certain whether the girls and this train journey have been, for her, merely a semi-conscious illusion or whether it is, after all, a question of events that really took place and of people she saw with her own eyes. At first, it is true, nothing really remarkable happens in the carriage. The girls are completely absorbed in the contents of their packages. The rustling paper reveals childish, perfume bottles in the shape of elves, modest white sets of underwear decorated with small amounts of lace, the gleaming toes of brand-new shoes and skin-coloured, East German corsets, which, respectfully, the girls call rubber panties. The smaller and livelier girl, who is wearing low-heeled school shoes, makes the bigger one, who has higher heels and lipstick on her lips, swear: 'We'll never wear anything else ever again! We'll always be in our rubber panties. They're just so good. You won't believe how slim they make your thighs!'

But the bigger girl is not so enthusiastic, although it is evidently precisely she who needs the help of the rubber panties. She responds accommodatingly: 'Mother certainly won't let us wear rubber panties in cold weather.' Now the smaller one slides closer to the bigger one and purrs persuasively: 'Let her! Do we have to obey her! Everyone wears rubber panties!'

For her, this extraordinary conversation brings interest and variation; it drives the sleep finally from her eyes, but also strikes the ear oddly, giving rise, in her sleepy head, to confused and unhealthy questions which would not have occurred to her earlier, before she knew the secret language. Out of sheer interest, she racks her brains for a moment without coming to any conclusion as to what 'mother' or 'rubber panties' might mean. 'Mother', 'rubber panties', 'thighs' and 'cold weather' sound, to what she considers her own rather experienced ears, so innocent that they may signify only very obscure and dubious matters. Evening walks, men with suitcases, anti-state ideas. What are the girls really talking about? She never finds out, for the girls throw her a suspicious glance, begin to giggle, and leave the train, tittering stupidly, at Valga station.

Are all those wooden houses, dust and drunken louts beyond the beer kiosk Estonia? Is the language spoken here in which the poem is written: *Marx is someone's staff, or Coué, another's triumphant rendezvous is cleaving flesh, bone, flee! But from what?* Is the air as cold and the evening as near as everywhere else?

As the train stands in the station, cold air flows into the carriage, filling it from floor to ceiling. Even her woollen jumper is no protection. Although she tries again and again to push her arms deeper into her sleeves and her collar further up her neck, her half-naked feet are still vulnerable to the draught. Some of her body-heat has also been absorbed by the knife and the key. But she will never get the lost warmth back from them. Nevertheless, she assures herself bravely that she is now free. Without the obligation to wait. Everything, both silence and words, let alone the clang of the doorbell and the sweetness of fear, was mere

107

mockery. Delirium and the hide-and-seek of shadows. A product of the imagination.

But how to turn tomorrow into a joke, or today? How to turn the key-word 'Estonians' in an encyclopaedia into a joke? How to turn the story of Abraham and Sarah into a joke? Is the parade in Red Square merely a joke? Or the Russian tank in Vaclav Square? And if it is not a joke, then what is it?

Even the Valga station building looks, at this moment, awkward and difficult to understand, a joke of an official nature. A crew-cut, cunning-looking little boy appears on the train; he resembles the hen-owner who stood beside the wooden fence in Riga. But the playmate of the Valga little boy is not a hen, like the Riga boy's, but a large, brightly coloured, garden pansy which, to judge from all the its distinctive markings, has been picked a moment ago from the flower-bed in front of the station. The pansy bed can even be seen from the carriage window as one looks out.

The boy plays with the flower as if it were a living creature, a kitten or a puppy or something rarer and perhaps even dangerous. And see, the flower's velvet gnome-face does indeed change its expression; sometimes it becomes larger, sometimes smaller, it sometimes grows darker and sometimes paler, it ripples in the boy's scratched fingers, his gnawed fingernails, like the blue bird which no one can ever catch, or the will-o'-the-wisp which lures travellers off the right road.

The boy mutters to himself; it looks as if he started his game before he got into the carriage, has identified with it completely and will not allow his new surroundings to disturb him in the least. When the train begins to move again, the boy flattens the mute face of his strange playmate against the dirty window and benevolently allows it to absorb its part of the prosaic details of the evening landscape as they creep past: the cow which, raising its tail, sullies the flowering side of the ditch, the old man who, for who knows what reason, shakes his fist at the train, the station toilet on whose wall is painted, without sparing the white oil-paint, the profound couplet: 'Dog arse furry / cat arse hairy.'

The little boy is not interrupted in his game even by the fact that two real longhairs sit down in the free places beside him, although their appearance gives rise to extraordinary interest in the other passengers. The carriage has filled up with people. Among them is even the Drunken Man who can usually be encountered only around station restaurants and canteens; he threatens anyone at all and adds with all his strength to the confusion and hubbub which has begun in the carriage as if by magic. The carriage of a moment ago, silent, cold, as if dead, is no longer recognisable. Among the muttering and the mumbling, swear words in Latvian, Russian and Estonian are clearly to be heard. Who is really uttering them is difficult to determine, as on closer inspection it looks as if all the passengers are attempting to hunch their shoulders and doze, their heads in the shelter of the coat hanging on the hook.

Nevertheless, the confusion merely increases. The Drunken Man lends it speed, letting out, at contracting intervals, boastful utterances: 'Up against the wall, all of you!' and 'Cut that hair, damn you!' The Drunken Man pretends to be stupider than he really is and identifies the longhairs sometimes as Jews, sometimes as gypsies, sometimes as Russian priests, and it is evident from everything that this is what he does for a living; this is not the first time he has amused his public with this turn. Those sitting closest to him gradually warm to his theme and begin in turn to incite: 'Yeah, that hair, shave it. Yes, now we'll take their hair.' The threats echo so encouragingly and in such a homely way that the longhairs themselves, who are the ones being shouted at, look as if they are used to them. They sit, neutral and interested-looking, as if they were at the cinema.

The Drunken Man yells, to please his audience: 'Bring me a knife! Damn, where can I find a knife and scissors! Now we'll get them, good and proper!'

Everyone laughs and grins, but no one starts looking for scissors. They merely look on and wait for what may happen next. The boy with the flower has left his game and lets his perplexed gaze wander from one face to the next.

But things develop in their ordinary way. The Drunken Man goes off to look for the scissors himself, and disappears. He cannot be heard or seen, and it as if *the grave has swallowed him up*. The tension does not, however, last very long; very soon it becomes clear where the Drunken Man is. Suppressed bellowing and loud thumping are heard from the corridor: the Drunken Man has got stuck in the lavatory and is now calling furiously for help.

The bellowing and thumping now accompany everything that happens in the carriage. No one pays attention to them. Especially since the Drunken Man's seat does not stay empty for long. At the same time a new main trouble-maker appears, sober and decent, wearing a white shirt and black trousers with a sharp crease and polished shoes. A real Man of the People, loquacious, with a gleaming gold tooth.

The Man of the People is more to the onlookers' taste than the Drunken Man. Here is a man who can be trusted. Some of them even know his wife, and that he has a motor pump in his well and many cubic metres of dry cladding timber in his shed.

Before the Man of the People manages to address himself properly to the matter in hand, the carriage attendant, a bony and brisk, moth-like woman, brings yet another man to the spot. He has a meaningless official title – he is the train chief. The man looks around him sleepily, and at first he sees nothing to interest him; it looks as if he sees preparations for *hair-cutting* almost every day, and hears the bellowing of someone who has been locked into the lavatory.

But all at once a change occurs in the train chief's face – his sleepy cat's eyes shine, his fleshy cheeks begin to move and his entire attention is directed toward the little boy who, swinging his legs and whisking his pansy from hand to hand like a piece of blue coal, follows the course of events unblinkingly.

With a quite peculiarly soft and creeping movement, the official takes from his pocket a hand which resembles not so much a human hand as an instrument made specifically for grasping and arresting, an industrially made tool, such as flat pliers. Handling this instrument skilfully, the official grasps the boy by the earlobe,

110

pulling him upright as if by accident, and asks mildly, even tenderly: 'And where are you from?' after which the boy sticks his stomach out valiantly and says: 'Over there.'

The man utters 'Aha' as if he has been expecting precisely this answer. Benevolently, he enquires further: 'And where are you going?' Just as valiantly, the boy answers: 'Over there!' But the official continues, with unwavering calm, with his strange conversation: 'Whose little boy are you?' Now the boy is confused for a moment, like a winged creature that finds itself in an enclosed space, a sparrow or a swallow or a putto who has fallen into a trap, and points to a figure in a grey jumper who is dozing, or rather pretending to doze, by the window: 'Hers!'

The carriage attendant explains to the train chief: 'It's not worth believing him. He travels with just anyone, and I've seen him before. That child certainly is a cross to bear! He just rides back and forth, and he cannot even be punished. He won't give his address. Even if you killed him he wouldn't!'

The official does not like the carriage attendant's words; his inscrutable gaze is already probing the dusty sandals and the over-large jumper whose collar covers a hot, blushing face. The eyes are squeezed shut unnaturally hard, like someone who is pretending to be dead. The official's gaze measures, classifies, commits the face to memory. Loses interest. One cannot immediately leap to conclusions from one glance. That capacity belongs only to the train chief, whose field is the uncovering and punishment of lawbreakers, not listing them.

In the detection of lawbreakers, the train chief receives a great deal of help from the man in the white shirt, who gives his own view of the disturbance, its nature and even its punishment. This is as follows: before the appearance of the *longhairs* in the carriage, everything was calm and quiet, really tiptop. The *irritating appearance of the longhairs*, however, annoyed the passengers, decent people and heads of families, and they demanded order and good behaviour. 'Taking into account the demands of the passengers,' the Man of the People spreads his hands, 'we cannot do other than to *cut their hair*.' As he gives his explanation, the Man of the People expertly and lustfully snaps a pair of long, steel-grey scissors humbly brought him by the carriage attendant.

But the train chief appears, whether he likes it or not, to be sleeping on his feet rather than listening to the explanation. He certainly does not exhibit any visible or palpable interest toward the *longhairs*. The chief's heavy gaze nevertheless continues to rest on the grey jumper-back and squashes it even flatter, crumples it still farther into the corner.

The only person who does not let a single word of the Man of the People's explanation escape him is the little boy, whose face is illuminated by such blessedly innocent amazement that everyone who sees it turns their face away as if they see, in that child's bright face, something frightening or forbidden to humankind.

Meanwhile, the Drunken Man has got out of the lavatory; he stands swaying in the lobby, shivering and grabbing at the empty air with his fists from time to time – hunting a buzzing dung-fly which he secretly believes, in the depths of his heart, to be the devil. The moth-like carriage attendant empathises completely with the devil-hunt, laughing until the nickel-plated crowns of her teeth are visible.

Just outside the walls of the carriage, the shore meadows and waters breathe, the mist is rising and the dew is falling. Perhaps, here, the old, golden, evening peace still reigns, calling the swallows to their nests, the cows to the barn and the children indoors. Are tension and waiting, broken windows and crumbling plaster, the dim glimmer of air-currents and the heavy hum of the future perhaps mere exaggeration and imagination, *over-dramatisation of the situation*?

Does not the Angel of the Lord over-dramatise the situation when he sets his hand on the wing-bones of young swallows and the vertebrae of lovers and finds, eaten into them, the lines: 'The purpose of persecution is persecution. The purpose of torture is torture. The purpose of power is power.' The Angel really does intend to begin prising them out with a knife and burning them with fire, but does he have any idea how many wings and backbones he would then have to crush and throw into the fire?

The forests groan, the engine whistles, the first, barely discernible, star appears in the heavens and the man in the white shirt invites the help of volunteers for the hair-cutting. The *longhairs* must be held still.

It is much easier than one might have supposed. There is certainly movement and tumult, but because the *longhairs* do not resist everything proceeds quickly, without tension or particular struggle. Faces are pressed against knees and arms twisted behind backs as if incidentally. If it were not for the fact that the *longhairs'* shirt-sleeves tear at the seams and come loose so that their bare shoulders are visible, there would be nothing at all to look at here.

Those who are holding them still, honest youths with smiling faces, are particularly fond of the phrase: 'Let's make men out of monkeys!' This they repeat time and again, and every time they hear it again from their own mouths it brings them renewed, childish joy.

The train is already slowing down. Past the windows warehouses, heaps and piles of cut logs, faded sheds and barracks, sagging outdoor lavatories, all flooded with the red light of evening. Now the man with the white shirt takes to his scissors. The loudspeakers in the ceiling begin to crackle and let out the cry: 'Next stop Tartu.' The boys who are holding the *longhairs* down fall silent and tighten their grasp; the muscles in their arms and around their jaws move, a gloomy and bitter smell of sweat spreads through the carriage. Suddenly the white necks of the victims are helplessly and intrusively bare. The cut ends of hair stick to the clothes of those nearby and eddy around their feet. They interest only the crew-cut little boy, who hurriedly gathers the longest and most beautiful locks, crawling between people's legs on the floor. He orders them into something resembling a bunch and then shakes it, satisfied and smiling.

But those who are leaving no longer have time to look at what is happening. In their excitement, they pull their coats and jackets

113

on inside out, and then have to take them off again, cursing. Some of them get ladders in their stockings; others cannot get their anorak zips to close. Children whine. Thoughts are elsewhere. Only the odd individual glance leaps from underneath the eyebrows to the bare necks of the victims, and turns away again at once.

The youths who were holding the *longhairs* down are already in the crowd of people getting off the train; they rummage in their pockets, put cigarettes to their lips and wait to get off the train. But the man in the white shirt finds it necessary to turn to the victims with an instructive speech: 'Do you Moseses think that it's fun for other people to shear your bushes, eh? If you want to try to live like Jesus, vermin, then, vermin, don't try to mix with other people. Piss off. Leave me alone, too. If you come anywhere near me I'll certainly have your hair.'

At this point the man in the white shirt pauses meaningfully and impressively, then lowers his voice and adds in a fatherly manner: 'If you're men, vermin, then fight back, don't mess about. Hit back, and then we'll be evens. I'll buy you a beer, too. But if you're girlies, damn it, then you should just have asked me nicely, you should have said, please, mister, don't do it, and nothing would have been done. I don't tease women, you know. Estonian women have always been well-dressed. Don't embarrass them!'

The man thinks what else he might say, then makes a decision and asserts belligerently, without any connection with what has gone before: 'You don't play around with the likes of me!' This confession does not excite anyone but the little boy, who has been following the words and gestures of the man in the white shirt with great interest and empathy. Probably the little boy believes that the last words of the man in the white shirt concern the bird in its nest, and tries to conceal the bunch of hair he has gathered from the floor behind his back. Who knows what he needs that hair for. It may be that, encouraged by Grimm's fairy stories, he intends to plait the hair into a rope which will allow him to find a route of escape always and everywhere. Even from the human heart.

The train is already stationary. The stopping time decreed by law is long, twenty minutes. The Drunken Man is asleep, snoring. But the *longhairs* suddenly brighten up; they do not listen to the man in the white shirt's fatherly epistle, but raise their hacked heads upright, shift the man in the white shirt out of their way as if he were a talking cupboard or a chair in trousers, and leave the train.

The man in the white shirt smacks his lips and falls silent. He snaps the scissors. Suddenly he notices something which he did not see earlier. His entire attention now pulls him toward a white neck which is sheltered by the massive collar of a grey jumper and thick, faded locks of hair. What the man in the white shirt thinks or imagines he sees in that neck and that hair, no one can know. All that is clear is that he wants to cut the hair, whatever the cost.

His adversary makes a belated gesture of self-defence, more out of surprise than out of fear. But it would be better if she had left it unmade. A tuft of hair has, in any case, already left her head; she will never get it back, and what is more, she pushes the scissors away so clumsily that they strike her own skin like the whip of the Lord. A bright red, delighted, insuperable trickle of blood appears on her white neck.

The man in the white shirt takes flight. Now the moth-like carriage attendant reappears, not alone but with a policeman. The policeman hesitates, but then grasps the sharp elbow clothed in the grey jumper and says, with boredom, his world-famous, worn phrase: 'All right then, let's go.'

9

The buildings do not yet fall down, the sky does not yet become a sea of fire, the seas and oceans do not yet overswell their limits. A cold wind blows. It raises goosepimples on firearms and drives rubbish and cigarette stubs to and fro along the oily asphalt.

The horizon behind the houses reddens so intrusively, so dramatically, that it feels of necessity as if the convexity of the Earth shelters not only the reserve areas around Tartu, the gravel pits and the notorious military airport with its transport planes readying themselves for flight, but as if the convexity of the Earth could quite freely also shelter the resurrected dead, escaped convicts, refugees betrayed to officialdom, all of whom have gathered in giant crowds and cover all the earth from the northern Arctic Sea right down to the Danube. They do not move or breathe. They are simply there. Waiting. They have time.

It looks as if, compared to what is happening on the other side of the horizon, walking with a policeman into a police station is child's play. Now would be a good opportunity to deploy all the unconsciously acquired information, gathered in cafés, to root theory in practice, to try for herself the various known forms of protest. She should criticise the policeman, throw the truth in his face, drag her feet, cling to tree-trunks, columns and poles, bellow like a wild beast and cry like a little baby, throw the policeman's cigarette stub away, burn the flag.

She doesn't have the heart for it. In fact, walking along, she is trying rapidly to resolve some existential riddles. She ponders her own heart and is amazed at what it has decided and where it finds itself. The trickle of blood is drying on her white neck, her trousers pocket is stretched by a penknife whose slippery handle is broken by the name LEV. The knife has a stainless blade which is not in any need of advertising: its quality is certainly known, it is always bright as a wound, or as love; it does not rust.

At the same time she invents a reason why it is not worth resisting the policeman. In her opinion, the policeman is not as he should be. He is not *proper*. A *proper* policeman should, according to her understanding and imagination, have been able to *frighten her a little* right from the start. He should have *hit* or *kicked* her. A proper policeman would step along the street in a different way, he would walk *stalwartly*, his chest out and his cap on the back of his head, not like this one – his steps stiff, his head weighed down, his epaulettes dangling.

For all this closed, sway-backed lifer cared, the *suspect* could quite freely quit, disappear like tin into ash or pincers into a well. Then work out whether she had existed or not. But in the eyes of the *suspect* all that looks unnecessary. In her opinion there are other, much more important matters, such as for example the mark of her own red mouth in clay or the meaning of blue cups in the secret language. It may therefore be said that over the blue cups she continues to pose, in her mind, a kind of heavy question mark.

The head of the suspect is, in any case, full of colourful, confusing and mysterious images, like the walls of an Egyptian grave vault. From among the other images, that of a white monkey rises forth with particular clarity: it has stretched out its paw and grabbed from the air a security-lock key and a pen-knife, pushing at them with its muzzle and trying them with its teeth before daring to play with them.

At this moment the city of Riga seems to her as dream-like and distant as her entire life until now seemed while she was there. Because while in Riga she did not believe that the word OVIR is also used in Tallinn or that plain-clothes men can be seen there, she does not now wish to believe that she heard those words in Riga at all. That she has even been to Riga. But if she has not been there, then why does she ask whether Kinski the dog is at this moment sighing and resting his chin on his paws? Why does she ask what Aunt Olga is doing and whether she is boiling the water for tea? Yes, and is the telephone ringing? Has the secret of the blue cups already been resolved? And what else will become clear?

Lost in these thoughts, her eyebrows rise, her eyelids remain unprotected, the corners of her mouth tremble. Is it the sternness of the evening light that surprises her, or is she surprised by the fact that pop music is audible from the windows, girls are giggling, children screaming, and of manhunts and plainclothes men there is not even a whisper? Everything is calm and quiet. Quite OK.

The police station door with its broken handle makes no impression on her. Like the policeman himself, it is not *proper*. It does not meet the requirements of a station. A proper station should have an interrogation desk, a bright, bare electric bulb and two chairs. Even a child knows that. A man in a leather jacket should be sitting at the table, in front of him a cup of tea or coffee. Tea is better. The man eats and drinks, but does not offer anything to anyone else. Thus theatrical and narrow-minded is her conception of the work of the organs of law and order.

She now finds herself in a room which brings her deep disappointment. It does not meet her expectations. If only it were in her power, she knows what a proper police station should look like. Disparagingly, she gazes at the table, which cannot with the best will in the world be considered a notorious interrogation desk. If the desk were not so scratched and full of splashes of glue, it could be mistaken for a table on which a mother irons laundry or kneads dough. At the very most, it could be used for making posters and banners or for laying out wall-newspapers. But there is no dough or wall-newspapers anywhere to be seen.

Across the desk drift dog-eared cardboard files, bottles of glue, paper clips and sweet papers. Cardboard files are also stuffed on to the shelves and into cupboards with grinning doors. A bitter and dispiriting smell of dust rises from the files and the cupboards. The cork covering of the worn floor is wavy and is full of matchsticks. Someone must have dropped a full box of them, and has not bothered to clear them up.

119

By the wall stand a few chairs with sagging seats and a long, brown-painted bench, like a coffin. From the side of the bench there hangs a piece of paper: 'wet paint', it warns. Two doors, which lead to other, unknown and perhaps more frightening, rooms, are closed. They look as if they are actually locked.

But from a behind third door, which is ajar, a moaning and a sighing are heard. Just as they should be. She has regained her certainty and remembers with enjoyment the slogans, old childhood phrases, that belong to this time and this situation: 'Fight and seek, find and don't give in! Better to die on your feet than live on your knees! It was I who brought you into the world, I who shall kill you with my own hands!'* Completely in harmony with these proverbs is a poster that droops over the coffin-shaped bench, announcing: 'For the good of all, for the happiness of all!' The heartbreaking moaning that can be heard from behind the door turns out, as she pricks her ears, to be more insignificant and ordinary than one might at first have thought.

Without waiting for the policeman to offer her a seat, she sits down, at her own initiative, on one of the chairs by the wall, moistens the corner of a handkerchief expertly with spit from her mouth and wipes the dried blood from her neck. She longs for a mirror and a warm tap. But from beyond the door the moaning goes on: 'Even home is worse than a dog-house! For God's sake! They bark like Alsatians! Take your pension from your hand right down to the last kopeck. What can I do about it, poor old thing. Even my feet hurt, it's like they're on fire as soon as those dogs come home.'

A muttering voice asks: 'Who? Who takes your pension?' Now the complaint gains strength like a snowstorm howling unbroken from one winter to the next. 'The boys. My own sons. Drink and rampage, like ravening beasts. Oh dear. It's awful even to think about it. I don't know what will become of them.'

Plaster falls from the ceiling; the light-bulb sways. Farther off, at the edge of the city, conscripts rise screaming into the air in crammed aeroplanes and head toward the south, Bohemia or Moravia. The rivers Vistula, Daugava and Neeme ripple as heavily as the rivers of hell. White mist rises from their black waters.

Only a couple of city blocks from here, in the shadow of darkness, Tartu University stands under a cold, sharp-rayed evening star, the building which, two or three years ago, caught fire for some unknown reason and burned like a beacon for the shipwrecked. It was an extraordinary fire. In the sooty snow, a long-dead professor was seen walking to and fro, his head bowed, his tie crooked. Then snow began to fall in large flakes, and snow covered everything. Only a few black, burned pages from books flew into the sky. Some books, however, were saved. But no one could save the spirit of the university. The spirit of the university burned.

Even without that spirit, the winter is survived. Summer comes. The rye fields sway just as before. Nettles and burdocks flourish. The as-yet-uncollapsed roofs of deserted buildings collapse. Lightning and rainbows are seen. At midsummer, the victory of light over darkness is celebrated with spirits and beer. Some people are fatally knifed, as usual, but some are also hit over the head with bottles. Shasliks are grilled over the midsummer fire for the first time.

The darkness of new winters falls, sighing, but it is already the unknown darkness of the future. One thing and another happens under its protection – children are kicked and beaten for anti-state slogans, everyone already knows what OVIR is, plain-clothes men are busy everywhere, in the heart of Tallinn the church dedicated to St Nicholas catches fire, and the fire is once more like a beacon for the shipwrecked. A cannibal begins to prey upon people who stay out late at night. The cannibal particularly likes thigh-meat; this he takes home to his refrigerator, teaches his wife to marinade it properly, and from time to time the delicious smell of stew spreads from the cannibal's house, tickling the nostrils of passers-by.

Some people know the cannibal's father; many know his wife. The father has a good education, and the wife is very beautiful. There is nothing to criticise in the cannibal himself, either – he has a good income, wears fashionable clothes, knows the latest jokes, takes his children to nursery school.

At the time of the cannibal's activities, the university fire has been completely forgotten. Now many people still remember it.

The windows shine greasily. The policeman has gone into a side-room and is squabbling there with someone else. The *suspect* has been forgotten completely. She shifts in her chair, squints at the window and tries to make out, in her murky mirror image, how the severed lock of hair affects her appearance. She decides at random, mostly to calm her own heart, that the difference is not great.

The *suspect* is tousle-headed, vigilant and alert. Seeing her sitting here, it is difficult to believe that the poet's bower is located in the garden of death. Or that a rose is a rose is a rose.

Suddenly she remembers the raisins which she stuffed into her pocket in Riga. Now she pulls them out and eats them. Then she tries once again to examine, in the window, the wound in her neck, but does not see anything. The wound reminds her of the woollen jumper neck, which, sore and uncomfortable, rubs her neck. With both hands, she tries to pull the collar away from her neck, to stretch it wider.

She is observed in these activities by the cleaner, who appears in the doorway with a bucket in one hand, a broken-off broom and a cloth in the other. The cleaner's chalk-white and bony old-person's legs, covered in thick blue veins, are bare. New black rubber galoshes gleam on her feet. No skirt is visible beneath her faded pinafore, just the legs of a pair of warm, salmon-pink, cotton bloomers. The cleaner dips the cloth in the bucket and begins briskly, almost angrily, to rub at the floor. As she reaches the figure sitting on the chair, she hisses, as if to a cat or a dog, 'Well, let me past.' But after a while she straightens her back, leaning on the broom-stick, groans and demands: 'Where did that Volli go?' Having gained in answer a hesitant and reluctant, 'I don't know,' she mimicks. 'Dunno, dunno... you don't hear anything else in this building, really you don't. Everyone gets up to all sorts of tricks, but if you ask who did something, then it's dunno, dunno. What did that Volli bring you here for today? This isn't a place for the likes of you. Should have taken you down to Timofyev. Or if nothing else then to Larissa.' From the cleaner's words, it is easy to gain the impression that the policeman called Volli brings the same suspect to the police station every day.

As she continues cleaning the floor, the cleaner waves her hands and talks non-stop. Even a silent listener seems good enough for her. Breathless from energetic scrubbing, the cleaner explains: 'Everyone has their cross to bear in this life. Just the other day a stray cat came in here, saw the safe door open over there and blow me if she didn't settle all her kittens down there. I knew immediately that it wasn't for the good. It was all my fault, after all – I hadn't noticed the door was open. Today there was another thing – since morning an old woman sitting in the corridor, just as if she was asleep. But a fiery bolt ran through my chest, and I thought, well, well, the old girl's kicked the bucket right here in the corridor. That's all we need. We've got enough to put up with without that. I go closer, look. I see that no one's dead here, this one's just snivelling quietly into the corner of her scarf. And it turns out – she doesn't dare go home, is afraid that her sons, pissed out of their heads, will attack her. Doesn't dare tell the policeman, is worried about her sons, of course. So she's just sitting there. I told her to go to Timofyev, said tell him, maybe they'll give your boys a bit of a thumping, frighten them a bit. Now, of course, it's all my fault – the old bag gets muddled up about what it is Timofyev does, only talks about her boys and doesn't go anywhere.'

After her monologue, the cleaner turns directly to the suspect and says, scoldingly: 'And what are you doing here, child? This is a pretty awful place. Yesterday they'd brought someone in who'd roasted his mum in the oven. Stuck her in the oven in pieces and then given her to his drinking companions to eat. Slept it off, then asked where his mother was. Mad as hatters, no one can do anything for them.' The cleaner looks around her and whispers judgmentally: 'Yes, do what you want to your mother, roast her in the oven if you want to, even though she brought you into the world... but then again – there was a man who sang to his mates, at the domino table, that Lenin was his uncle and Stalin was his aunt, and Beria was his bride, and for that he got the sack and was stuck in the loony bin.' Apologetically she adds: 'It's just what the women at the graveyard say, I don't know if it's true. Volli said who knows...'

The very same Volli appears on the spot and gives the conversation a new direction. The cleaner scolds cosily, without trying to curb her language in any way: 'Volli, didn't I tell you just this morning not to leave anyone sitting here, just send them all to Timofyev? Let Timofyev learn from experience the trouble you have with them. Let him be ordered on to the train like a little boy.'

Meanwhile, the policeman paces to and fro in the room. From the cupboard to the window and from the window to the cupboard, and every time he passes the figure sitting on the chair she feels the presence of sorrow and melancholy. The policeman's uniform does not suit him at all; moreover, the coat is visibly tight, and pulls across the back.

The cleaner's unabashed grumbling does not provoke any kind of echo from the policeman. A heavy silence develops in the room, finally broken by an order from the policeman: 'Take some paper and write a report.' The cupboard door creaks. A thick piece of greyish paper appears on the table. 'Write – I, so-and-so, travelling from A to B, hereby state that I am not the culprit for the breach of law and order that occurred on the "Chaika" train and consider the event a misunderstanding. Signature, date and domicile.'

And that is all the policeman has to say. But even from this the cleaner takes courage and praises him: 'Such knowledge of human nature that Volli has. He knows at once who's a crook and who's just the victim of wicked tale-telling or informing.'

The policeman whimpers and wrinkles his eyebrows. Smokes for a while, silent, and then gives the surprising, dull and wearworn order: 'You may go.' It is clearly visible that the policeman's thoughts are elsewhere and that he scarcely even notices what is happening in this room. The cleaner, on the other hand, notes everything, does not leave anything unseen, although she, too, is silent for a long time, then mutters something to herself. Both of them, the policeman and the cleaner, seem rather suspicious.

Because the *suspect* feels that not everyone in this room is in possession of their full senses and because she is so very disappointed in the police station, she rises decisively to her feet, pulls up the collar of her jumper, which is rubbing her neck more sorely, and makes for the door.

But meanwhile power has shifted entirely into the hands of the cleaner. The policeman's words, 'You may go', the cleaner condemns completely: 'Drive a young child out on to the dark street just like that, would you? With drunks and villains. Is that the reason you dragged her here on the basis of wicked talebearing.'

Quite surprisingly, the cleaner announces: 'Now I'm going to make just a little bit of soup. It's not much, but a person has to eat.' Having said this, she turns completely to the figure standing by the door and murmurs: 'We don't even know if she has a train ticket in her pocket, the poor little thing, and hungry, too.' Then she steps decisively toward her and warns: 'What did I tell you – don't go out in the street alone. We'll take you to the station. Just wait, wait a minute, and I'll heat up some soup.'

From the darkness under the table the cleaner produces a small hotplate that has seen better days and switches it on. There is no protective plate on the coil, and it begins to glow red. Into the cold and dreary room, filled with cigarette smoke, there spreads in a moment the breath of life, a drowsy and fatiguing warmth.

Now the cleaner trots into the corridor. On her return, she has in her hand a small, water-filled aluminium pan which she sets on the glowing hot-plate. After that, from the endless darkness under the table, there appears a jar of cheap, thin vegetable soup, and the cleaner opens it with some difficulty, because the tin top of the jar is completely rusty. The policeman follows the laborious opening of the jar with indifferent eyes, almost as if frozen solid, and does not even raise his eyebrows.

When the water is chattering to the boil, the cleaner pours in the contents of the jar and says, comfortingly: 'It'll soon be ready.' The policeman's chin droops still further toward his chest. He nods heavily in rhythm of his thoughts like an old horse, and the large black shadow of his head moves on the ceiling with the grey steam from the cooking. It seems uncomfortable and somehow creepy. Everything is different from how it ought to be.

Because she has heard that it is not worth resisting *mad people* and that one should not quarrel with them, she sits down quietly, at the urging of the cleaner, in her former place, draws her feet neatly under the chair and waits to see what will happen next.

The world shifts from its place, life slips into emptiness, it curls up and fits inside her chest. Until now she has believed that she can get by without pronouncing the final and fateful words no and yes, by postponing choices. Final and fateful choices she has, until not, believed to happen somewhere quite different. Either on the battle-lines or in salons. Either in St Petersburg or in Paris. They demand particular conditions and begin at some time specially reserved for them, like films or exhibition openings.

It is a complete surprise to her that, regarding tomorrow, she must make a decision quickly, without any fateful ceremony, sitting on a wobbly chair in a police station, her arms in gooseflesh, in the steam from the soup, accompanied by the monotonous and unclear mutterings of a completely unfamiliar old woman. Then the decision is made. She will not continue her journey to Tallinn, but will return to Riga. To announce her final fate. Nothing more. The world returns to its former place; it rolls off her chest like a black ball. After the decision, breathing is pure joy and exultation.

She hears again what the cleaner is saying, nodding from time to time doubtfully herself as a sign that she is listening. The mumbling continues: 'Tomorrow they'll be bringing Toomas back in a zinc box. Makes your heart break just to think of it. Volli, have you remembered to book an undertaker?' The cleaner turns toward the policeman, who nevertheless says nothing in answer; he has covered his face with his cap and appears to be asleep. The cleaner wipes her eyes and continues: 'And you can't talk to anyone about it. Volli won't listen. I brought Volli up, you know. His mother was my cousin. Alma, that's Volli's mother, was buried in Russia. Who knows where her grave is. I took the boy in. He's been a good son to me. Like a little adult right from the beginning.

'We didn't have much in the way of money, or much to eat, but he put himself through school. Went to the police academy. Got his uniform and bread free there. Got a start in life. Took a really good wife. Toomas was their only child. Just took him into the army, and now he's dead already. That's what it's like, human life. Killed his parents' only child. Do you feel good now? Beasts! Yes, and for Volli it's meant that he's not the same person today as he was yesterday.'

The cleaner confesses, whispering: 'Do you know, when Toomas was in the first form he stopped going out into the playground and didn't want to go to school. Cried so terribly that the others taunted him on account of his father. And it was true, the child wasn't telling a lie. I heard it myself once – the boys told Toomas to say stop, say stop. So the idiot went and said stop, and then they said ha ha ha, your father's a cop, your father's a flop, and all sorts of things like that. Volli began to think of leaving the police force. But how do you do that when that's what your life is built on. It was hard on Volli that an innocent child like that suffered on account of his father.' The cleaner blows her nose and ends her long narrative with surprising curtness: 'It takes all sorts, whether you're a policeman or what; the main thing is that you should keep your human heart.'

But suddenly she falls completely silent and listens to a distant, barely audible howling, which could with goodwill be thought of as the rumble of an aeroplane but which could also be something completely different. The galoshes on the cleaner's feet crunch threateningly. When the rumbling draws nearer and becomes louder, the cleaner mutters mysteriously: 'Out of there, on your way. Just take other people's sons there to kill.'

The vegetable soup is boiling, bubbling. Into the dark red,

steaming eddy of the soup fall black, heavy curses that have been passed on from one generation to the next: 'Home then, marsh dog, home then, earth dog, home then, fire dog, home then, water dog, home then, man dog, home then, boy dog, home then, blood dog and your three pups.'

Then the cleaner says in a quite different, dull voice: 'The soup's ready now. Fit to eat.' The policeman coughs behind his hand and begins obediently, humbly and mechanically to slurp from a twisted aluminium spoon.

Shadows move on the walls. She no longer has the faintest idea what the time is. It looks as if three travellers from ancient times have coincidentally gathered by a campfire, and the only thing which unites them is the curse.

The rails rumble. Through the thick darkness pass trains whose freight carriages conceal zinc coffins, within them dead bodies killed in the service of the State. It cannot yet be known which will reach its destination first, the zinc coffin and body or the sparkling disc of the sun, which is also on its way here.

10

If one is entering a strange apartment without permission, it is not worth hesitating. It is no doubt for that reason that she slips through the dark crack of the door so swiftly. Not like a human being, but like an animal or a spirit.

She has opened the lock quite differently from how she had thought, easily and completely soundlessly. She squeezes the now unnecessary key hard in her hand. She does not know what to do with it any more. The hallway and its greenish twilight recall an empty bottle or an underwater kingdom. It shows that the curtains in the rooms are still drawn. The tinkle of glass beads, which answers even the tiniest movement, is also as it was.

Since everything is as it was, why does she not take a step forward? For whom is she watching – and, moreover, with such tension, her calves cramped, her heart, her throat and her eyes glowing?

In the rooms, the floating smell of fresh floor-wax mixes with lemon and peppermint, cologne and the strange, scarcely discernible scent of toothpaste. Nevertheless, the nervous clatter of Mother's heels, Aunt Olga's heavy, thumping footsteps and the scraping of the claws of Kinski the dog are nowhere, yet, to be heard. Neither does Father glide soundlessly along the newly waxed parquet toward the hall, in his head unguessable, secret thoughts that originate from the other side of the Iron Curtain.

Lion opens the living-room door. Life-size. Flesh and blood. The expected one himself! Both jump back and remain standing, their hands on their breasts. So much breath has never been held by one mouth. Neither has so much breath ever been breathed from one mouth.

Because no one has warned them of this moment, they are quite helpless before it. But the angel of this hour stands alone beside the coat-stand, hidden by the coats, and looks on with interest to see how they will negotiate it. Extraordinary how hard their ribs are. Even after this moment has passed, they are still whole. They were not, after all, squeezed to pieces or cracked to smithereens!

Their teeth collide and they see sparks before their eyes. They are on the point of suffocation, but they do not suffocate. They have been almost choked to death, but they are still alive. Finally, all at once, they draw a deep breath and begin busily to lick the bitter, salt water from one another's eyelids. At the same moment their noses become moist and begin to run in the most prosaic way. They wipe their noses energetically on each others' shirt collars.

It is quite impossible to make out whether the only word they use is 'Ah', 'Oh' or 'Well'. Who knows whether the word exists in any human language at all. It is unclear whether it is only a patch of light of unknown origin that slides across the wall, or if it is really the white monkey, which creeps forth from behind the clay box pulling strange faces and grinning with its teeth. It waits for a suitable moment to touch their eyelids curiously with its paw, although the coins which it expects to find there turn out, on closer inspection, to be nothing more than kisses. Disappointed, the monkey hides again. But it is not worth losing vigilance! Who knows at what moment the monkey will reappear. But it may even now be ready to jump, beating at the wall with its tail and licking its muzzle.

Even so, they merge with one another's skeletons. They are not hindered by the enriched lead or tin or frightened by the amount of radioactive material in their tissue. The salt in their blood sparkles; the gold and iron glow.

Even the dust-particles have come to life: they have risen from the dust of the earth, dance in the air and form columns of light, which slowly, together with the sun, move through the quiet rooms like the world of the dead. The sky, which can be seen through the slits in the curtains, now higher and more distant than ever before. But the clouds, which still hang in the sky, look as if they are made of cardboard, gilded and hung on pieces of string. As soon as it is necessary, they will be pulled up again.

In the room, nothing can as yet be heard, not even the breathing of the sleepers. Their faces are frighteningly and cruelly happy. They belong quite completely to the future, before which every even slightly more serious sorrow, not to mention suffering, seems ridiculous, childish and trivial, a mere round zero.

What is certain – the hour whose last moments are now at hand will not disappear anywhere. It will merely move. It will travel back and forth in time, and everyone will be able to rest their foreheads for just a moment against its sparkling edge.

Now this hour is already moving onward, toward other lovers. But these ones here turn back toward reality and open their eyes. They awake trembling in the same way, as if a cold Baltic breaker has thrown them on to the shore. They even shake themselves like wet dogs. Burst out laughing. But there is nothing to laugh at here!

In the end, at last, Lion gets his own notebook and penknife back. Although he has decided not to ask, he nevertheless asks. Asks quickly and as if it did not really matter: 'Where were you?' The other responds equally quickly, and again as if it did not matter: 'In Estonia.' Unspoken words and questions without answers are already giving signs of their existence, not yet on the tip of the tongue but distant in the depths of eyes.

For the moment, they are still easy to rebuff. One only needs to turn one's head to one side and squeeze one's eyes shut, and this is just what she does. Lion's face lights up. It seems as if Lion is seeing those eyelids and that face for the first time. For a moment he covers the squeezed-shut eyes with his hand. Under his fingers, he feels the defiant, moving wing-flutter of the eyelashes. Now Lion takes the head in a strong grip between his hands. Looks from every side, turns and twists, inspects it like the work of his own hands or the fruit of his own thoughts.

The scissor-wound that blemishes the neck Lion cleans quickly and efficiently with his lips. Before he glances at it again, the naïve, ancient, secret hope of miraculous healing flares in his eyes.

Seeing clearly that his kisses have not healed the wound, a peculiar expression, concentrated rather than melancholic, appears on his face, as if it were necessary for him, at this time and this place, immediately to begin to reshape that head. Seemingly part of this new attempt is the way in which he blows aside the locks of hair which have fallen into her eyes. With concentration, he blows straight into her eyes as if he were carrying out some particular task, summoning a spirit or awaking a clay form to life.

The sun shines half-obliquely on to the television and conjures up on its empty, dusty screen a ball-shaped shadow which, with goodwill, it is possible to believe to be an image of a celestial body, for example the Earth. Who knows what is already happening on its surface at this moment.

The zinc coffin sent on its way from Prague has, at any rate, reached its destination. Even the funeral has already been held. The grave mound, whose clayish earth is decorated by a few wreaths and crooked vases of flowers, cannot, fortunately, fracture the breathtaking beauty of history. The leaves on the trees turn upside down in the wind. Everything moves, trembles, changes, disappears and appears once more.

Now Lion can do nothing but uncover the half-forgotten clay form that stands in the corner; he must look at it. He also directs a proprietorial glance towards the clay box. He is pleasantly surprised on finding that Aunt Olga has not yet forgotten to dampen it. Even the unfinished work is not yet as dry as he might have feared.

'Yes. Now I know what I must do!' Lion announces profoundly after turning the statue toward the light. He looks at the solidified form of the clay as he has just been looking at she who lives in flesh and blood.

No one can know what Lion's eyes see just now in the clay. In any case, he says, as if he has just made Lord knows what discovery: "Courage!' And see – that hollow phrase suddenly takes on great power, it struggles in his chest, burns his palate and his tongue. It is not in the least impossible that it will also be able to change the future.

When they now look into one another's eyes once again, it happens in a different way. With the merciless, dazzling gaze of victors. The gaze announces with complete clarity that if they can only transform all their love and their sorrow into words soaked in blood and images awoken with breath, not even a silver bullet will hit them. Why grieve! Why should they care about distances of thousands of kilometres, the convexity of the Earth, even if it should separate them for ever! Why should they care about the State or its killing machine, even if they themselves are up to their neck in its craw. What is it to them!

For this reason it is very amusing and moving to see how seriously they approach this day. It can even be asked whether they are not trying altogether too hard in their seriousness. As now.

All one can do is marvel at the sincerity with which Lion presents his account of his journey to Moscow and how thoroughly sympathetically she listens to his descriptions of people and places which should not move her in the least.

His hands already wrist-deep in clay, a clay-dust apron on his clay-spattered overall, Lion continues his story and moves around the uncovered statue, gradually changing the expression on its face. Holding pauses that are sometimes shorter, sometimes longer, and energetically mixing the clay, Lion thus also succeeds in conjuring forth Leo's office in Moscow.

Leo is sculpted from a single piece of stone – take it or leave it, like a pharaoh. He has wide shoulder-slabs and an angular granite head which reflects all the burning lamps of his office in turn. When Leo turns in his chair, he does so heavily, with his entire body.

His eyes, on the other hand, are lively and bright. They move from Lion's face to the black official telephones on the table, which seem bigger than natural size, and back to Lion's face. There are no more than three telephones, but all the time it feels as if there is a whole flock of them. Their bawling constantly interrupts the conversation. 'Don't imagine that they *rang*. No, they *bawled*,' Lion emphasises.

In a word – Leo has, with his glances, clearly given it to be understood that it is certainly not worth speaking seriously in this office, whatever one's business is. Leo himself speaks mainly of Aunt Olga's youth. Into the gaps between the bawling of the telephones, however, Leo slips a quick glimpse of his own kidney-stones and their recent operation.

Leo benevolently condemns Lion's first name, considering it idle snobbery and running after fashion. On the other hand immediately, and under Lion's eyes, he reads the letter Aunt Olga sent, and is delighted by the old, faded photograph enclosed with it. Moved, he also blows his nose more than once. But after reading the letter, Leo steers the conversation to his own kidney-stones once more. Finally comes out from behind his desk, he shakes Lion by the hand and says: 'Come to our house this evening, and we'll have a *game*,' emphasising: 'Chess loves patience, my dear friend, patience.'

The word 'game' intrigues Lion; he ransacks his brain for its real meaning until evening, without results of any kind.

In the hallway, Leo's wife, *Aunt* Loora, begins immediately to remember a story about a visit by the six-year-old *Lev*, long ago. The story goes as follows. Little *Lev* does not eat or drink, stands by the window, holds on to the curtain with both hands, and cries. He is asked what is wrong. Little *Lev* answers: 'I'm sorry for Aunt Olga.' 'Why?' 'Because Aunt Olga is a woman and can never smoke a pipe like Comrade Stalin's.'

As long as *Aunt* Loora speaks, Leo stands by the door of the guest room, clicking his fingers and waiting for the right moment to start laughing. The two doors are opened and look – in the room sits none other but Kuzminitchna, life-size, with her glasses and her earrings, *surprise surprise*. Kuzminitchna is cheerful and kindly, sips at some oriental tea that has been prepared just for her and *makes* proper conversation. That Kuzminitchna is a friend of Leo's was not known even by Aunt Olga, who knows everything. In a home setting, Kuzminitchna radiates like the sun and shines like the moon. She thanks and thanks her host as if she could never thank him enough. Promises, first thing tomorrow morning, to collect all the emigration papers and use them *where they should be used*.

There is a serious worry, too. For Leo cannot, apparently, on any account, influence the staff of the Latvian military district. Just recently, Leo has personally criticised the Riga officials of excessive liberalism in the matter of military service. Although Leo is sure that only military service makes a youngster into a man, he nevertheless understands that *in this case* it would merely be a hindrance to emigration. 'And I recommend emigration,' Leo whispers mysteriously. 'I have it from certain sources that our future is very gloomy,' he warns.

In this case what is needed, apparently, is a proper, foolproof diagnosis, which will be recorded on all the documents. And so Leo has given *Lev* a letter to his old Latvian friend, a doctor of the rank of major.

'A heart problem will be best,' Leo comforts Lion as they say their farewells. 'Heart, remember, heart,' he shouts, standing in the doorway, into the night's darkness after Lion.

This, after all, is the *blue dinner-service* about whose possible purchase the boy was recently informing his mother in such gloomy tones.

It turns out that there are also great conflicts of principle in the family. Aunt Olga, apparently, does nothing but dream of the vineyards of Thurgau and longs to walk there with her beloved brother. She tells Kinski the dog about their future days in Thurgau. Lion's mind, since childhood, has contained nothing but the stones of Jerusalem. All Mother's graves and relatives, on the other hand, are in New York. Apparently Father laughs bitterly about the stones of Jerusalem. This time he has even said, 'I decline to comment,' and that is all. Father even takes a scathing attitude to the canton of Thurgau. It is only through *force of circumstance*, apparently, that Father can tolerate the canton of Thurgau, which does, on the other hand, have *excellent rail connections to the metropolises* but in which there is altogether too much nature.

In Switzerland, there in Thurgau, only the smell of milk, apparently, hovers in the air. Cows trample wherever they possibly can. Neither is there any shortage of cockerels or of hens. The balconies are full of flowers, which demand constant watering. It is not worth even standing for a moment by a pond, as the water in the pond immediately begins to seethe and all the fish swim to the shore. They open their mouths and demand balls of dough, all kinds of *bran and crumbs*.

Only in New York, apparently, can a person find shelter from nature. 'Do you hear! Only in New York!' Lion confirms, as if in revenge on himself. The blood beneath his skin glows for a moment, his eyebrows grow together at the bridge of his nose into a single black line, his teeth bite his lip defiantly. To judge by all of this, Father's future life is not likely to be very rosy.

Father has today flown from Moscow back to the canton of Thurgau. 'Perhaps he is still in the air at this moment,' Lion surmises, somewhat idly. It looks as if he is much more worried about Mother, who is expected home from Moscow this evening. A shadow moves across Lion's face. He makes an attempt to eye his own work with Mother's eyes. More clearly. More critically. More challengingly. He wrinkles his eyebrows. Walks round the completed sculpture, inspects its shadows with the vigilant eye of a bird of prey. When he finally raises his eyes, they gleam with the joy of the victor. It is for that reason he swallows down so courageously the life-question that has risen to his lips. He forcibly takes, from the god of destiny, a little more time of grace. Pushes her fingers into the clay. Squeezes them so hard that the bones crack. Hard, like a comrade in battle.

Then he says, with peculiar amusement: 'Look, Father sent you a present,' and places in her hand a Swiss penknife exactly the same as his own. Adds in explanation: 'According to Father, you are just like this knife. There is a lot inside your head, but nothing can be seen from the outside.'

The face of the receiver of the gift goes red. Just as intended. They burst out laughing simultaneously, as if with one mouth. Use it as recompense for all their unlaughed laughs. Slap their knees with their hands and snort. Sway on their feet. Hang helpless on each others' necks and then bounce back.

Everything that exists exists only in order to allow them to laugh. Laughter forces the brown plait of hair in the bathroom cupboard to open itself, bend by bend, and to straighten itself, as if it had got the idea of crawling into the room with the laughers. The plait's destiny is now set, and it cannot escape it. By spring it will be in the place long ago determined for it – the earth of Grandfather's tomb.

The laughter resounds as far as the bedrock of the Karelian isthmus and the stones of Jerusalem – it shatters the bones of the fallen of the Winter War and the medium-range missiles of the future that are aimed at Jerusalem as well as the tank columns of today, which fracture the surface of the streets and crush people's shinbones. That laugh can quite easily free even glass mountains and the sea of fire on the other side of the horizon.

And see, a miracle – with the help of that carefree laugh, they succeed, as if it did not matter, in uniting their own life and destiny. When, twenty-three years later, there arrives a January afternoon when the sky shakes, the distant but clearly recognisable shape of a black celestial body appears of itself, as if by magic, on empty screens and all radios babble at once about the Holy War, the Mother of All Wars and the beauty of weapons, then they are, with today's laughter, flesh of this morning's flesh and bone of this morning's bone. That morning has a distant predecessor, all ages are flung together and who is at this moment in Jerusalem, who in New York and who in Tallinn is of no import. They have laughed the power and importance of distances into oblivion today.

This laughter is interrupted by who else but Kinski the dog with his turbulent greetings. Aunt Olga is standing at the door. Kinski expresses his joy largely by attempting energetically to knock both Lion and Aunt Olga over. Kinski takes run-ups for higher and higher leaps. His broad boxer's cheeks shake, the whites of his eyes gleam, wild and cheerful. Even Kinski's white chest seems to have moved, in his excitement, from his throat toward his neck. 'Kinski, enough already! Bad dog Kinski, bad dog!' Lion has to raise his voice.

But Aunt Olga looks on this unexpectedly unleashed rumpus feeling quiet satisfaction and emotion. To hide her tenderness, she pretends to complain: 'The floor just polished, and look, it's full of clay! You don't visit the studio, that's just another new fashion! And they call it life!'

In her bag Aunt Olga has a large fish, a live carp. It must be killed, cleaned and boiled in milk until it is soft. For milk-carp is Father's favourite. As always, Aunt Olga intends to celebrate Father's departure with an impressive lunch. Even unseen, Father will have his place at the table, as ever.

So today Aunt Olga has a great deal to do. She does not really know how she will get it all done. Nevertheless, Aunt Olga is in a particularly bright mood today. Her face would serve as a living illustration for those who do not know what the phrase 'lit up from within' means. She does not tire of confronting Lion with questions, although Lion told her everything yesterday. She enquires about what Leo had to say about his operation, what Aunt Loora was wearing and whether Father ate all his fried chicken or only the legs, throwing the rest away, as he once did.

From time to time Aunt Olga interrupts her important tasks, appears at the living-room door and confesses: 'That's certainly a weight off my mind!' Strange that she does not, at the same time, childishly clap her hands. In Aunt Olga's eyes, Lion's call-up papers have, for today, completely lost their threatening authenticity, as she fixes all her greatest hopes trustingly on the unknown doctor of the rank of major. Aunt Olga's most important subject of conversation for the day could be condensed in two official and dry words – family unification.

Aunt Olga's trust is frankly astonishing, for as she next appears in the living-room doorway with her cries of joy she suddenly calls waggishly: 'Come along now, my girl, and give me a hand. Hold the fish by the tail!'

But Lion chases Aunt Olga impatiently back into the kitchen. As if he were afraid that she really would go and hold the fish by the tail, Lion takes her head between his hands like a dog's head, leans his forehead against her forehead, his eyebrows against her eyebrows, his eyelids against her eyelids. The terrifying question is made up of the most ordinary words: 'Well? Will you come with me?' To which she shakes her head without a word. I will not.

Perhaps they would have stood like this, unmoving, unbreathing, forehead to forehead, in this door opening until the end of the world, if it were not that the fact that Kinski the dog suddenly takes the initiative, raises his massive muzzle to the roof and begins to howl in his morose bass. Otherwise the building is silent. As if dead. There is no sound even from the kitchen. When they reach the kitchen, the Angel of Death is already there.

Aunt Olga is lying by the door, the fish's head in her hand, a joyful smile on her face. Beside her on the floor lie the two halves of the great fish, gleaming and threatening as Moses' tablets of the law.

Although their faces turn white and their legs falter, what of it? They can howl their grief properly. What is it to them?

A lost forest bird, far from its home, looks in through the window and cries in its echoing, mocking voice, straight from the house of Solomon: 'Set me as a seal upon upon thine heart, a seal upon thine arm...'. and flies, humming, on its way, as if it had come such a long way only to make mockery.

The murky water of the great rivers flows heavily and unswervingly, like blood along the sides of the earth, down to the darkness of the oceans. The sun comes closer and closer and presses its divine face against the window. The glass beads in the ceiling tinkle although no one is arriving or leaving. The quite particular and very promising gleam of the tank columns, the aircraft wings and the tram lines is extinguished.

The sky takes on its proper form once more. It becomes a dome and a vault. Everything is still ahead. Including the future, and its terrifying beauty.

Notes

8 The first line is a common slogan from Soviet times. The second is a famous slogan from Lenin's day. The third dates from the years following the Second World War.

11 Russian: 'the fact is'.

14 Russian: shop where goods are sold on commission, widespread under the Soviet regime.

14 The Visa and Aliens' Registration Department.

15 A free quotation from the Estonian poet Mihkel Mutt.

15 'Just you wait': catch-phrase from a popular Russian television cartoon.

43 'Schlachta': the landed aristocracy of Poland.

53 'the Ulmanis period': Karlis Ulmanis, prime minister of independent Latvia several times between 1918 and 1940. He was also its fourth president, 1936-40, after he merged the offices of prime minister and president in the aftermath of an unconstitutional political coup in 1934. (Ulmanis permitted his predecessor as president, Alberts Kviesis, to serve out his term of office.)

58 Paul-Erik Rummo (b. 1942): an influential Estonian poet who made his debut in the 1960s. With the exception of the quotation on page 15, all the poetry quoted in the book is his. In the autumn of 1992 he was appointed Minister for Cultural Affairs in the new Estonian government.

84 A reference to two etchings – 'Cabaret' (1931) and 'Hell' (1930-32) – by the artist Eduard Wiiralt (1898-1954).

85 *Kapos*: criminal prisoners in German concentration camps who were used as overseers and low-grade guards.

120 The first quotation is a common slogan used by Komsomol, the 'Communist Union of Youth'. The second is a slogan from the Second World War. The third is a famous quotation from the epic poem *Haidamky* (1841), about the rebel leader Taras Bulba, written

by the Ukrainian author Taras Shevchenko (1814-1861).

Afterword

Spring in Prague, Winter in Tallinn

by Richard C. M. Mole

On 20 August 1968 five hundred thousand Soviet, Polish, East German and Hungarian soldiers invaded Czechoslovakia on the orders of the Kremlin to crush the Prague Spring. Alexander Dubček, the reformist First Secretary of the Czechoslovak Communist Party, had attempted to create 'Socialism with a Human Face' by abolishing censorship, liberalising the economy, rehabilitating political prisoners, giving the National Assembly a more prominent role and promising open, multi-candidate elections. While the Czech population responded excitedly with public assemblies and lively debates, Moscow watched the developments with considerable unease. Not only was the *cordon sanitaire* between the USSR and the West at risk of fraying but the events in Prague were having a discernible effect on the Western borderlands of the Soviet Union, most notably in the Baltic States. With hindsight, the Soviet leadership was right to be worried. Just over two decades later the USSR would be brought to its knees by events set in train by Estonia, Latvia and Lithuania, three small republics whose national identities and desire to regain their independence failed to be crushed by fifty years of occupation.

   In its entire history Estonia has only been in control of its own destiny for little more than thirty-five years. Given its strategic geopolitical importance, the small nation was occupied over the centuries by Denmark, the Teutonic Knights, Sweden and the Russian Empire before finally achieving sovereign statehood in 1918. This period of independence was short-lived, effectively coming to an end on 23 August 1939 as a result of the Molotov-Ribbentrop Pact signed by the USSR and Nazi Germany, a secret additional protocol to which assigned the Baltic nation to the Soviet sphere of influence. While during World War II Estonia insisted it was committed to a policy of neutrality, Moscow used the escape of a Polish submarine from Tallinn harbour as proof that it was unable militarily to defend its neutrality and therefore pressured it into signing a 'Pact of Mutual Defence and Assistance'. Subsequent relations between Moscow and Tallinn were, if not harmonious, at least peaceful until 15 June 1940, when Soviet Foreign Minister Molotov accused Estonia of violating this Pact by entering into a military alliance with Latvia and Lithuania, which, he claimed, was directed against the USSR. He thus issued Estonian ministers with an ultimatum: allow Soviet troops free access into Estonia, arrange for the resignation of the Estonian government or face a Soviet invasion. They had little choice but to give in. On 21 June a left-wing government friendly to the USSR was formed in Tallinn, and in July elections were held to a new national assembly, with a single list of candidates and no permitted opposition. The programme called for alliance with the Soviet Union, a purge of representatives of the former regime from state and municipal posts, increased wages, social insurance and the distribution of land to landless peasants. On 21 July the newly elected National Assembly voted unanimously to join the USSR, a request that was accepted by the Kremlin on 6 August 1940. The British Foreign Office, echoing the sentiments of the majority of Western states, refused to recognise the annexation of Estonia.

In the summer of 1940 Andrei Zhdanov was sent to Estonia to oversee the Sovietisation of the new constituent republic. Forcing it from capitalism to socialism and then communism would, so the architects of the Soviet state believed, produce new social institutions and in turn generate new cultures and identities. By the time Estonia came under Soviet control, the USSR had been subjected to Stalinist nationality policy for the best part of two decades. While initially a policy of 'national in form, socialist in content' had been pursued, allowing socialism to be promoted within an ethno-cultural framework, by the 1940s this had been largely abandoned in favour of naked Sovietisation. This social engineering project had two objectives: to destroy bourgeois social structures and introduce a new social organisation, and then remove 'the remnants of bourgeois ideology'.

Demolishing Estonia's pre-Soviet structures was a straightforward enough task. The Soviet authorities simply nationalised its industrial, commercial and financial sectors. Removing 'the remnants of bourgeois ideology' proved more difficult. To the authorities the greatest threat to Communist ideology came from pre-Soviet national elites, attitudes to private property, 'religious superstition' and manifestations of nationalism. The national elites that had not fled to the West during the war or been exiled were immediately replaced by pro-Soviet communists. Following the annexation, many Estonian communists who had emigrated to Soviet Russia during the period of Baltic independence returned to their homelands to head up Soviet agencies or simply to take advantage of the better living conditions. However, the authorities distrusted anyone who had not undergone twenty years of Sovietisation, which meant that even the local communists were not fully trusted and political control had to be exercised by force and terror. 10,205 people were deported to Siberia in a one-week period in June 1941 alone. That same month Nazi Germany invaded the Soviet Union, reaching Estonia by July. Initially, the Germans were welcomed as it was hoped that they would rid Estonia of the Soviet presence and restore the nation's independence. However, it soon became clear that this was not going to happen and Estonia remained under German occupation until 1944, when the Soviet Army forced the Germans to retreat.

Regaining control of Estonia, the Soviet authorities sought to win the support of the local working-class population, by offering them the chance to gain important positions in society, thus instilling the idea that they were promoting social justice. The new regime also used the education system as a means of ideological indoctrination, introducing a system of crash courses, whereby adults who had left school after primary education could obtain the eight years of secondary schooling in three. This injected large numbers of the proletariat into the educated classes and created a new elite of Soviet supporters, watering down the power of the traditional establishment. Similarly, special academies were set up to train barely literate people within just a few months to act as economic managers, judges, lawyers, etc. While the vast majority of Estonians still opposed their new rulers, the authorities did succeed in converting several thousand citizens to the Soviet cause and thereby creating a Praetorian Guard.

In time, however, even the most avid supporters of communism came to see the dichotomy between Soviet theory and practice, a state of affairs of which the authorities were only too well aware. One of the first manifestations of this 'breakdown in ideology' was the suicide in November 1946 of Johannes Vares-Barbarus, the chairman of the Soviet government of Estonia, who took his own life on having become disillusioned with the system he had helped to set up. Assuming that most indigenous Estonian communists felt the same way, the regime carried out a large-scale purge of indigenous political figures in 1950-51 and by late the following year there was not one home-grown ethnic Estonian among the four Estonian Communist Party secretaries and twenty-six ministers, all of whom were replaced by Russians and Russian-Estonians.

While assuming control of Estonia's political and economic structures, the Soviet regime also set about eliminating private property, cultural manifestations of nationalism and 'religious superstition'. To eradicate private property, it imported the system of collectivisation to the new republic. Although the Soviet authorities had initially promised owners of medium-sized farms that their property was safe so as to secure their support, large farms were split up and distributed among peasants with little or no land of their own. The land belonging to refugees who had fled to the West was seized and redistributed. The land redistribution programme was completed in 1947. From 1948 a number of party directives appeared encouraging the 'spontaneous' creation of collective farms (*kolkhozy*). Glowing reports of life on *kolkhozy* in other parts of the USSR had been appearing in the local press since 1946. The process of collectivisation in Estonia was slow, however, with only 5.8% of Estonian farms having been collectivised by early 1949. Frustrated by such slow process, the authorities brought pressure to bear in the form of mass deportations. In a period of just a few days from 20 March 1949 some 60,000 people were deported from Estonia. Following the deportation of 10% of all Estonian farmers, most of the rest joined up voluntarily. By the end of 1949, the percentage of collective farms jumped from 8% in March to 80%.

The educated Estonian elites – the bearers of national consciousness – were hardest hit by the flight of refugees to the West. By 1946 half of those with a university education had left. Nevertheless, the titular populations did retain control of education and culture as the need to speak the local languages precluded Russians from taking up these positions. However, the gaps in the fields of economics and technology were quickly filled by mainly Russian immigrants. While most immigrants were unskilled labourers, thousands were officials assigned to manage and supervise factories. The peak influx period was 1945-47, although immigration continued steadily thereafter as the authorities forged ahead with their industrialisation programme. Between 1945 and 1947 180,000 non-Estonian nationals arrived in the northern Baltic republic, with a further 33,000 following in the period 1950-53. The indigenous share of the population fell from 94% in 1945 to 72% by 1953.

Expressing national identity through art and literature was all but impossible as mass culture was channelled through and controlled by Houses of Culture, whose directors were chosen for their political sympathies or their ability to be indoctrinated. Of the writers that remained after the war, few were productive and most of those who did produce were criticised for the

147

content of their work, for depicting only the past and writing work filled with grief or sadness. In the last years of Stalin's rule writers and playwrights came under pressure to produce in Russian or were purged not for criticising the Soviet regime but for being politically neutral.

In the field of education, the Soviet authorities had new textbooks written by 1945. Those printed during the period of independence were banned. Teachers were retrained according to the Soviet system or brought in from other parts of the USSR. Universities suffered most from the exodus to the West. There was a desperate shortage of lecturers and at the same time the number of people attending institutes of higher education rocketed, encouraged by the new regime, which used the education system as a means of ideological indoctrination. The history of Estonia and the Baltic region was rewritten to highlight the positive role played by Russia, while the history of the Communist movement was rewritten to deny Balts – even prominent Marxists – any signs of initiative. Instead, they were portrayed as being the willing beneficiaries of Russian leadership. As history was taught from an exclusively Marxist-Leninist perspective, the incorporation of Estonia into the USSR – which was 'greeted with great pleasure' by the Estonian proletariat – and the mass deportations of the fifties were described as being instigated by and carried out for the benefit of the exploited workers. However, the attempts by the authorities of the USSR to create members of a Soviet nation by rewriting Estonian history failed, as the official histories provided by the Soviet education system clashed with the history Estonians were taught at the kitchen table.

By the final years of Stalinist rule, tens of thousands of Estonians had been exiled, murdered or fled to the West, many thousands more faced abject poverty as a result of collectivisation, manifestations of national culture were repressed and religious institutions persecuted. Unable to express their national identity, most Estonians internalised their aspirations to national independence and opposition to the

Soviet regime with the result that they became profoundly alienated from the society in which they lived. Even the pro-Communist minority came to see that their hopes for social justice had failed to materialise: there was less freedom than before and greater injustice, poverty and mass deportations; the class struggle – which had been used to justify the erosion of national and individual rights – had failed to produce a better life.

The death of Stalin in 1953 ushered in a period of greater relaxation in political, economic and cultural life in the USSR as a whole and in the Baltic republics in particular. In addition, Beria and Khrushchev's power struggle in the Kremlin resulted in their attempting to curry favour and gain support among the leaders of the national republics, thereby granting them greater political leeway than hitherto fore. Attempts to ethnicise the republican cadre were officially supported by the Central Committee and tacitly endorsed by Moscow. The result was the dismissal from positions of power of those non-native Estonians who had failed to gain a command of the local language. The Estonian Council of Ministers even criticised the policy of economic interdependence as this prevented the use of local raw materials, led to local specialists being sent outside the republic and resulted in an influx of Russians. The improved psychological mood produced more open – albeit timid – expressions of patriotism, such as the wearing of EESTI instead of ЭCCP on sporting strips. Religious and national holidays from the 'bourgeois' era were also celebrated, albeit without official sanction.

In an attempt to secure symbolic legitimacy for its rule, the republican regime also courted the indigenous scientific, academic and cultural elites and attempted to include focal points of native patriotism in Soviet commemorative practices.

The massive psychological boost that Khrushchev's denunciation of Stalin had given to the more nationally minded politicians in Estonia prompted many Russian functionaries and labourers to leave and encouraged a number of émigrés to return. By 1959 the indigenous proportion of the Estonian population had gone back up to 74.6%. Writers, artists, filmmakers and scholars sought to exploit the thaw that followed the death of Stalin to reassert national values and expressions of national identity, although they were still restricted by the outer limits of Soviet nationality policy. Nevertheless, new styles and structures replaced the rigid formulae of the Stalin era and, more significantly, Socialist Realist content was widened to include subjects such as guerrilla war, deportation and the negative impact of collectivisation. Estonia experienced a wave of 'new' genres, such as surrealism, theatre of the absurd, abstract art, avant-garde, jazz, national folk-songs and modern dodecaphonic experimentalism.

Once Khrushchev no longer had to court the republican leaders, however, his attitude towards native culture, language and autonomy underwent a sea change. From 1957 his pronouncements on nationalism and religion and his encouragement of the process of *sliyanie* (merging of different nationalities into a Soviet nation) left little doubt as to his true colours. In 1958-59 the 'voluntary principle' on Russian schooling was introduced, whereby members of the titular nationality were given the option of sending their children to Russian-language schools (although many aspects of this principle were, in fact, non-voluntary); from 1958 the number of years non-Russians could receive education in their own language (especially in higher education) began to fall; pressure was placed on Estonian and other non-Russian writers to publish only in Russian so as to hasten assimilation; and in 1959 a number of non-Russian leaders were purged for 'national deviation'. Nevertheless, compared with the period of murder and exile, the late 1950s and early 1960s were years of hope, particularly following Khrushchev's overthrow in 1964. His successor, Leonid Brezhnev, slowed down the former's rapid assimilation policies and spoke more of *sblizhenie* (nations becoming closer but still separate) rather than *sliyanie*. Oppression continued but each small advance gave the

Estonians hope for the future. This hope died in 1968.

The invasion of Czechoslovakia was followed in the USSR by a period of stagnation and social alienation that was to last until the late 1980s. At the same time, the process of assimilation accelerated, the number of trials for national deviation increased, the number of non-Russians in high office fell, even in their own republics, and the teaching of Russian as a means of bringing about more rapid assimilation intensified, with lessons in the language starting in nursery school. While Estonians did not suffer more than other nations in the USSR, they were forced to endure terrible hardships at the hands of the Soviet regime. The social engineering project introduced in 1941 destroyed existing social structures, resulting in the expulsion or deportation of national elites, the confiscation of private property and the banning of religious worship and the cultural manifestation of nationalism. Soviet nationality policy led to the deportation of tens of thousands of Estonian men and women, collectivisation, purges, Russification, political violence, economic stagnation, environmental pollution, mass immigration and a massive shift in the demographic make-up of the republic. While these measures and the feeling of injustice at having been annexed by the USSR stoked nationalistic feeling among Estonians, their desire to express their national identity and the desire to re-establish an independent state had to be internalised due to the immense power of and climate of fear generated by the authorities. While the desire for independence never died, Estonians would have to wait a further twenty years for it to be fulfilled.

HANNE MARIE SVENDSEN

Under the Sun

Written in 1991, *Under the Sun* is the story of Margrethe Thiede, the daughter of a lighthouse keeper in an unnamed small fishing community on the north-western coast of Denmark. We follow Margrethe through her childhood, her years as a student in the capital, her marriage to a mentally unstable man, her involvement in the peace movement, and her old age.

The novel is also about a changing community where fears of violence at sea and rampant commercialism on land are strong undercurrents. The building of a naval base and the ominous presence of foreign submarines intimidate the fishermen and their families, and an accident caused by one of these intruding vessels forms the catastrophic climax of the novel.

The storytelling is funny, playful and clever. Dreamscapes and fairytale worlds blend with realistic narration to form a Danish brand of magic realism. The author explores central questions about the relationship between language and constructed worlds, about time and space, and about the nature of fiction.

ISBN 978 1 870041 62 1
UK £9.95
(paperback, 302 pages)

For further information, or to request a catalogue, contact:
Norvik Press, University of East Anglia (LLT), Norwich NR4 7TJ, England
e-mail: norvik.press@uea.ac.uk
or see our website:
www.norvikpress.com

Lightning Source UK Ltd.
Milton Keynes UK
UKHW021256260122
397711UK00006B/188

9 781909 408272